A KISS FROM A GARGOYLE

KISS FROM A MONSTER SERIES
BOOK 7

CHARLOTTE SWAN

eBook ISBN:

978-1-960615-17-6

Paperback ISBN:

978-1-960615-18-3

Cover Design by Charlotte Swan

www.authorcharlotteswan.com

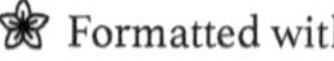 Formatted with Vellum

To everyone who believes love is stronger than stone (and if you had a crush on Goliath from the TV show Gargoyles growing up, this is mainly for you)...

CONTENT WARNINGS

For a full list of content and trigger warnings please go to the author's website.
www.authorcharlotteswan.com

WILLOW

Rain lashes at the windows of the carriage.

The grand wheels of the contraption navigate the uneven road without delay. Each bump along our journey nearly sends me clattering to the floor. I manage to steady myself, unwilling to break the heavy silence between my fellow carriage patrons and me.

Daring a glance from under the heavy wool of my hood, the stoic faces of Father Knoll and Sister Grayvle remain unchanged as we continue our journey. They could be siblings—both with severe, dark eyes and deep wrinkles around their mouths. While the majority of Sister Grayvle's hair is covered by her white veil, I've seen her auburn tresses before, and they bear a striking similarity to Father Knoll's.

When my eyes trail towards him, I find his gaze already searing into mine. I drop my stare as goosebumps erupt on my skin. I say a silent prayer of gratitude that I'm alone on my side of the bench. Beneath this scratchy, threadbare robe, I am naked. My state of undress is a punishment for my crimes. As is the blood red fabric I'm currently draped in.

It is a far cry from the pristine white robes I've worn for the last twenty-one years of my life. I hardly recognized myself in the color. Sister Grayvle had said the color suited my kind better—in her eyes, I was never deserving of the white robes of the Sisterhood of the One True Faith.

To her, I was always what I am now—a hedonistic beast who deserves to be cast out of the only home she's ever known. To be shunned and disavowed—left to rot by the side of the road as all vermin should be. The word impure rings through my head. It's the only thing the other Sisters said to me as I was stuffed into this carriage and sent off to God knows where.

I suppose the word wasn't untrue in my case, but one can hardly blame me. As an orphan, abandoned on the steps of Thorncatcher Monastery, I was adopted by the One True Faith before my first birthday. I took my first steps before the altar, and my first words were prayers. I should've been the most pious of all my Sisters. I should've looked up to Sister Grayvle as a beacon of what true servitude to our One True God could give me.

As I grew older, it became apparent to everyone that I was different. Restless, the Elder Sisters would call me. My mind would often wander during prayer. I was curious in a way the other girls my age were not—or at least they were better at hiding it than I was.

A few of the sisters even whispered I was cursed by a demon—my heart filled with a salacious nature that only more prayer could absolve me from. It was all for not, though. No matter how hard I prayed, my soul longed for more. As I grew up, it led me to do things that were unthinkable to the other Sisters.

I would sneak in contraband—books, dog-eared and forgotten. They were filled with tales of bravery and adventure. Themes of love and good triumphing over evil bled from each page. My rebellion first drew breath from inside those pages.

Hidden amongst the travels and treasures of battle were scenes that changed everything for me.

Lust-filled depictions of couplings unlocked a world I had been barred from.

I'd huddle under my sheets, using the flame of one spare candle to devour each delicious sentence. My skin heats just thinking about my favorite passages—of a knight returning from a deadly battle, near the brink of death, only to be restored by his lover, the princess. In her embrace, he is whole, and they are one.

I savored each passage over and over, memorizing my favorite sentences by heart. From those wanton pages, a seed was planted within me. I would find that type of love—my heart yearned to be bound to another. I would experience the same euphoric, bone-shattering pleasure, or at the very least die trying.

Those books remain back at Thorncatcher Monastery, tucked under a loose floorboard. While they may no longer be with me, the messages inside them are carved into my heart. They are more than just stories to me. Reading those books taught me about the world beyond the monastery. It showed me things I never would've otherwise.

It showed me that love was not forced but given freely.

Love is a tenet of the One True Faith. We are raised to love our God, our Sisters, and, of course, our Blessed Fathers, like Father Knoll. We are given no choice in the matter, merely told that is how we should feel. It is our payment for the safety and security His Love gives us by being pious and loving towards our Father. This love is familial—any romantic love is seen as sinful. Sisters are to remain chaste and untouched until death.

The type of love I was reading about was forbidden to me. Perhaps that is why it entranced me. My path to damnation was set the moment I read my first indecent page. I had to discover what it felt like to have someone else's hands upon me—to share breath with another in the darkness of a bedroom.

I had to start somewhere. My twenty-first birthday had come and gone, and I was no closer to discovering pleasure than when I first read those books at fifteen. I was feeling more restless than usual that day in the garden. The feeling of my life slipping away behind the walls of the monastery forced me to reclaim some of the freedom they stole from me.

The young man from the neighboring town had just been convenient. I had kissed him in the middle of the garden with no preamble. There was no effort on my part to hide what we were doing. His lips had been soft, but surprise had rendered him mostly motionless. By the time he started to kiss me back, we were being pulled apart. He had not been my first kiss, and I hope he won't be my last. It was nothing special, and my loins were not left burning.

The man had been dismissed without pay, while I would be forced to suffer for my lecherous actions. It didn't help my situation that Sister Grayvle had discovered us.

The Elder Sister had been singling me out for years. She would chastise the shape of my body once I began to grow into my curves. She'd call them obscene and make me wear double the garments to hide my shape. My prayers were never up to her standards. Any attempts I made at rededicating myself to the One True Faith were met with her dismissal.

She was almost purring as she dragged me towards Father Knoll's study. My begging was met with stony silence as she tossed me inside. It had not been the first time Sister Grayvle had sent me in there to deal with Father's wandering hands and foul breath.

It had never gotten too far, but it was only a matter of time before Father Knoll stopped being patient. His desire for me was more than evident, and the thought of him touching my naked flesh made me want to vomit. For as much as I loathed her, I was relieved I wasn't making this journey with only Father Knoll.

His condemnation of me had been swift inside his study. There was anger in his beady, dark eyes that nearly stole my breath. He had proclaimed that if I was willing to give myself so freely to a stranger and forsake God, then my punishment would be for my sinful flesh to be on display for all to witness.

A punishment that far outweighs a chaste kiss that wasn't very good.

It mattered little; I was stripped in the great hall before the eyes of all my Sisters while they chanted *impure* in unison. I was given these sinner's robes and loaded into this carriage without so much as a backward glance. My punishment was to begin immediately. The nudity hardly bothered me. As Sisters, we bathed communally; it was not as if it was a sight they'd never seen before.

Truthfully, I've barely had time to process it all. My stomach rolls with each shaking bump along the road. The journey through *The Woods* had been short enough. Stories about it being filled with unholy magic and depraved creatures were well-known. We were forbidden from travelling into it at Thorncatcher Monastery. However, I had ventured into it many times and found it no more frightening than any other forest.

That's not to say *The Woods* are not special. I have seen many things inside them that the True Faith has no explanation for. Perhaps that is the real reason they do not want us wandering too deeply into them.

The carriage lurches to a harsh stop, almost sending me to the floor of the compartment. Without hesitation, Sister Grayvle pushes open the door. Both she and Father Knoll take my arms in their iron grips and pull me out into the pouring rain. Instantly, I am soaked to the bone. My robe clings to me, and dark hair falls into my eyes.

The only thing I can see is a crumbling building, the door

nearly falling off the hinges. Apprehension makes me plant my feet. I thrash in their grips, refusing to move any further. If only I could escape them—make a break for it and finally—

"Behave," snarls Sister Grayvle. "This can always get worse."

Her words find their mark, and I go limp. I have been trained to obey her commands, and no matter how much I want to fight, my body isn't listening anymore.

Father Knoll huffs at my side but offers no other words. The scent of alcohol mixes with his body odor and nearly upends the contents of my stomach. I shake my head, focusing instead on where they are taking me.

As we approach, I realize this is no ordinary building. It is a church—one that has seen better days. It is a modest structure with a tall steeple pointing towards the gray sky. The windows are busted in, and the door hangs from rusty hinges. The steps are nearly completely rotten.

"Where are we?" I ask in a trembling voice.

"Silence," Father Knoll snaps.

For the first time since we left on this journey, fear grips me tightly. My heart hammers painfully in my chest. The scent of wet grass and rotting foliage nearly chokes me. Darkness begins to cloud the edges of my vision. I do not know what awaits me inside. We are beyond the monastery walls. There are no rules here. I am completely at their mercy, and I'm frightened.

As much as I long for my freedom, them casting me out for my transgressions is not an option. They will not simply let me go. I am a ward of the One True Faith—their property. A runaway dog that needs to be reminded of who owns her.

"Please," I whimper. "I'm—I'm sorry. Mercy, I beg. I'll be good. Please!"

"Quiet!" Sister Grayvle roars.

Together, my two captors yank open the crumbling church doors and pull me inside the dilapidated structure. Once inside, the two whirl me in front of them. Father Knoll's eyes are bloodshot. Raindrops glide along the deep grooves of his heavily jowled face.

"Your soul is polluted with sin, Sister Willow. You reek of it," he spits. "Some time spent in Shadowveil Church should help remind you of your place. You will be remanded here for three days and be given no water, no food—"

His eyes swirl with heat. In one fluid motion, he grips the front of my robe and yanks it off me. The threads snap easily. The fabric all but disintegrates in his hand. I scream as he bares my flesh to his lecherous gaze. A tremble starts in my hands that soon consumes my whole body. I try to cover myself, but Sister Grayvle holds my hands bound.

"No clothing of any kind," he continues. "As humble as a beggar, maybe once you are reminded that you are nothing, you will be grateful to me for the life I've given you. You should think about that while spending your days and nights begging God for forgiveness."

Sister Grayvle shoves me back. I stumble on an uneven floorboard and fall against an overturned pew. Her thin lips twist into a haughty grin.

"Whores deserve to be punished," she sneers.

My chest feels tight as I watch her snatch up my robe and walk towards the open door. Father Knoll stares at me for a moment, his eyes licking over every inch of me. I can see him weighing the decision. Bile races up my throat as he takes one small step forward.

"Father!" Sister Grayvle calls. "Come before it's dark."

Father Knoll groans, licking his lips before slinking away. The danger he presents is still there. I can't even bring myself to feel relief as the door slams shut. The light from outside is faint. It bathes the uneven wooden floorboards in pale yellow light. The ceiling above consists of decorative arches and stained glass. There's a chill inside the church that makes me shiver from my place on the floor.

Any thoughts of escape are quickly squashed by the sound of nails being hammered against the door. The light drains as the gaps in the slats are mended by heavy planks of wood. Each slam of the hammer rattles through the barren church. With each nail struck, my punishment becomes all too real.

Sitting in the darkness, I will the stinging in my eyes to dissipate. There has to be another way out of here.

Still, even if I found it, I have no money, no allies. I am a woman—a naked woman—all alone in the world with no connections. I may be naive to life outside the monastery, but I am no fool. It would be ignorant to believe the only people I would run across in the neighboring town would have my best interests at heart.

Even still…I can't just sit here.

Maybe there is something I can use to set myself free, and that will also double as a weapon. I have to try—at the very least, find something to protect myself in case Father Knoll decides to come back.

With a steady breath, I rise to my feet. This is an older church, like the one on the grounds of Thorncatcher. If I remember correctly, there should be living quarters for a few Sisters and a Blessed Father behind the altar.

In the dark, I have to focus on each step, careful not to trip over a forgotten candlestick or broken board. The last thing I need is to injure myself. The aisle finally begins to taper up towards the altar. Without thinking, I look up and immediately wish I hadn't.

A scream rips from my lungs at the figure awaiting me at the center of the dais. A demon—straight from the pits of hell —stares back at me. A gargoyle is encased in marble. Its large maw is open, showing two rows of extra-sharp teeth. Its hands end in deadly claws and are extended forward as if to make a grab for me. Large wings, tipped with two sharp claws, strain from his muscular back. They fan out behind him as if in mid-flight.

I cannot stay here. Not with that thing present, I'll take my chances back at Thorncatcher. With a scream still stinging my ears, I turn from the gruesome sight and run towards the door. Throwing myself onto it, I bang my fists against the unyielding wood.

"Let me out! Please!" I scream. "Sister Grayvle! Father Knoll, please! You cannot leave me here! Please. Please!"

The only sound that greets me is that of the hammer. Once it falls silent, my stomach sinks as I hear the carriage door rattle open. A few moments later, there is a crack and the clacking of hooves trotting far away from this church.

I hadn't realized I was crying until hot moisture splashes on my chest. The scent of dust and smoke fills my lungs. As my vision blurs, I see my reality for what it is. I am trapped here. Trapped with a monster who, even if petrified, will find some way to devour me. Why did I have to be restless? Why did I have to wonder when the others did not?

My life would be so much easier if I were pious like my Sisters. Why would God give me this curious spirit if I was meant to live my life in a cage? What sins could I have committed to be dealt such a punishment?

I begin to sob in earnest, chest rattling cries that make me slink to the floor. Wrapping my arms around myself, the temperature inside begins to plummet. The sound of the rain outside is quiet in comparison to my wails.

There's a chance I could escape, but where would I go? Another monastery wouldn't take me in. To be abandoned by the True Faith is to be abandoned by all. That sentiment has never rang more true than it does to me now. I have nothing—I am nothing.

I should be brave like the heroes in my story. I should have faith like the princess locked inside a tower. She never lost hope that her rescuer would come save her. Am I not in a similar predicament as her? My knight could be on his way to save me right now. I cannot give in to despair. I will find a way to survive this. Besides, it's not as if—

The sound is soft at first, the shifting of stones against each other. I hadn't heard it over my cries, but as my tears begin to dry, the sound intensifies. There are sharp cracks that echo down the aisle. Snaps soon follow in their wake, followed by the loud boom of stones crashing onto the wooden floor. The ground below me shakes, and my eyes widen as I take in the unholy sight before me.

The gargoyle remains unchained—mouth open, claws extended. However, its stone prison is breaking. Hard marble gives way to gray flesh covered in sparkling scales. White light streams from between the cracks. A scream crowds my throat, but I can't make a sound.

I'm powerless to do anything but watch as the final crack sends the remaining marble crashing to the ground. Striking blue eyes sear into me, and my scream breaks free.

2

____

BAEZAL

It was her devastating cries that had finally awoken me.

The sound of her agony turned my stone prison into dust. The first thing I saw when at last my eyes could move was the tiny human woman huddled against the old church door. Fear made her muscles stiff. She had turned shockingly pale.

In contrast, I had never felt more alive.

There was a sensation brewing inside me. It was primal and all-consuming. Confusion was still present. As was the potent sadness that threw a cold bucket of water on me. Being cursed to remain a statue but watching the world change around you creates a distinct type of hopelessness.

I have many questions about this new world I find myself in. It has been nearly a century since I walked amongst the living. No longer the silent observer, I long to see many of the sights time had nearly stolen from my memory.

However, there were more urgent matters pressing me than a need to glimpse the sea.

How many of my kind remained? Where was the True

Blessed Father who had cursed me all those years ago? My rational mind wants me to believe him dead, but with his ability to wield dark magic, I wouldn't be surprised if the bastard had managed to cheat death.

I should be punching through this rotten ceiling and setting out to fulfill my revenge. Yet, the only moves I can seem to make are towards the tear-stained angel shaking against the door. I hadn't even realized I'd left the dais and was now close enough to touch her. The scent of lavender and wildflowers fills my lungs. I greedily inhale more of her, grateful that all my senses have returned so that I can fully appreciate her.

My sight is perfect. I can see every inch of her naked flesh. She tries to cover herself with her hands and the tresses of her long, mahogany hair. Her beauty is undeniable. A restlessness crowds my heart, urging me to take her in my arms and shield her from every present and unseen danger.

She is far too delicate; this world is unkind and would see her loveliness marred by its cruelty. The need to protect her is strong. I've never felt like this towards another before. An over-whelming sense of primal need nearly sends me to my knees before her.

I had presided over her kind for decades before I was cursed. We were made as protectors, meant to serve as eternal guardians over the Sister of the One True Faith. That was until the True Blessed Father had seen our protection as a slight against him and his rise to power. We would've been the only force strong enough to stop him, but it was too late to act.

With one decree, he bound us into our stone prisons. Some managed to flee for a time, but in the end, it didn't matter. Before this church was abandoned thirty years ago, word had come that no gargoyle remained amongst the living. Each one of my kind was entombed the way I had been.

That fateful day returns to me as does the True Blessed

Father's proclamation. The only way my kind had the chance of breaking from our stone prisons was if God saw fit to put our fate on our path. If we discovered our True Fate, we would be freed.

Whoever this human is, she's important. She is the thing that saved me from eternal damnation, and I will do everything in my power to figure out why. Why has God entwined our fates in this way? Why is she here, of all places, and why is she naked?

The two figures who had left her here and stripped her— one an Elder Sister and one a Blessed Father—had reeked of cruelty. Most humans did.

The one at my feet did not. She smelled of sweetness. I hungrily inhale more of her scent, allowing it to settle into my blood. A delightful shiver runs through me.

Innocence shrouds her like a veil. All young Sisters have it —growing up in an isolated monastery tends to create a naivety. However, inside her angelic body lies a soul filled with wickedness. Not a perchance for evil, but of desire. An inferno of lust roars within, in need of being carefully stoked.

Is that my fate then? To be the one to stoke her flames of passion. Surely I cannot be that lucky. When I had roamed the land freely, I had had my share of enjoyment with mortal women. Ones paid handsomely not to mind our physical differ- ences. My wings pull tight at the notion, and the woman whimpers.

I must be scaring this innocent creature.

That cannot truly be my fate, to bed a virgin sister? While I would certainly enjoy it, the fear tainting her lovely scent tells me she would not. I would never disregard her wants in the face of my own desire. It is enough to just be close to her. She has freed me from my curse, and for that I will always be grateful.

There has to be more to this—I am certain of it.

Another whimper puffs from between her full pink lips. Her dark eyes are wide as she stares up at me. Long tendrils of damp hair cling to her chest. Raindrops collect in the hollow of her collarbone. My mouth waters at the urge to drink from there. I clench my muscles and snarl at myself to get a grip.

Opening my mouth, I find I cannot make a sound. The small human curls more in on herself, bracing as if she expects me to strike her. Whoever has harmed this fragile woman will pay for such atrocities. Swallowing against my dry throat, trying again.

When still no sound comes out, she flattens herself as far against the wall as she can. As my silence persists, I grow impatient. Snapping my wings back, my feet leave the ground, and I float back towards the dais. She whimpers again, eyes snapping shut. I don't like the scent of her fear. Maybe this will help her see that I am not a threat.

Snatching up a discarded sheet covering one of the altar tables, I hold it out in front of me and approach slowly. The material is rough—not at all good enough to touch her perfect skin. Vowing to get her something warmer later, I pray she takes the covering. Hopefully, this will help her relax.

My steps are slow as I approach. The only sound is my claws clicking against the wooden floorboards. I try not to crowd her as I get closer. Blinking open her dark eyes, she stares up at me. She is far too pale for my liking. Extending the sheet towards her, she eyes it warily.

Raising a small hand, she takes the corner of the sheet in her trembling grasp. I let the material flutter to the ground and watch as she quickly wraps it around herself, covering her skin from neck to ankle. She snuggles into the fabric as if it were silk and not threadbare cotton.

Swallowing thickly, her eyes connect with mine. The scent of fear is slowly receding, though not disappearing altogether.

"Thank you," she whispers.

Her voice is a hymn—sweeter than any melody. It is the sound of a chorus of angels reaching from the heavens and pulling me into their warm embrace. The soft sound washes over me and settles into my heart, solidifying the fact that she is my fate. She is meant to be mine—in whatever capacity she deems me worthy.

Those two words have bound us together, whether she realizes it or not. I will do anything for her—she will never have cause to feel afraid again. I will honor and protect her until the world around us crumbles into dust.

Silence stretches, and she grows apprehensive again. I lick my dry lips, still feeling remnants of stone clinging to my dry skin. I must speak before I lose this first opportunity to earn her trust.

"Ba...Ba..."

I press a claw into my chest, hoping she understands. Her dark brows lower as her full lips twist downward.

"Bad?" she offers.

I huff, shaking my head. My wings flap behind me in irritation.

"Ba...Bae...Baezal."

Pointing at myself again, her eyes travel up the plains of my chest back towards my face.

"Baezal," she repeats, and pleasure tickles the base of my spine. "Your name?"

I nod.

Untucking her hand from the sheet, she holds it against her own chest. Her brown eyes sparkle in the dim light.

"Willow."

The word washes over me.

"Willow," I say back. The word is sweeter than wine. "Beau—beautiful."

Color blooms high on her cheeks, and though it seems

impossible, she is even lovelier than before. Ducking her head, dark hair falls forward and covers her face. I want to reach out and tip her chin up, but that would be unwise. Her fear is beginning to leave her, and I don't want it to come rearing back.

"Thank you, again, Baezal." She holds up a corner of the sheet. "I'm—I'm sorry about how I reacted. I've just never seen a—a—"

"Gargoyle?" The hoarseness of my voice is beginning to lessen.

"Yes. I've only heard the stories of how, um, dangerous you can be."

I would laugh at the absurdity of her statement, but that seems unwise. Given our history, if there is anyone to fear here, I should be scared of her. Still, her words give me pause. Admitting to me that she has been taught to fear me is a step in the right direction. I at least hope it is. In time, she will see she has nothing to be afraid of.

"Do you believe these stories?"

Willow bites her lip. Emotions flit through her dark eyes so quickly I can hardly keep track. With a sigh, she rises from the floor, tucking the sheet around her. Have ankles ever been described as beautiful before? Willow's certainly are. She's been handcrafted by angels into perfection.

"Honestly," she says. "I'm not sure what to believe anymore."

Taking a small step towards me, her head barely reaches the center of my chest. She cranes her neck back all the way to keep our gazes locked.

"Father Knoll has remanded me here to sit in humble prayer to repent for what I've done." Her words give me pause, but I don't dare interrupt her. "He will return for me in three days, or at least so he says. I wouldn't be too shocked if he left me here to die."

"Never," I growl. "I will protect you—keep you safe. It's my job."

Willow blinks at me, stunned at my declaration. Silence stretches between us for a moment before a small smile curves her lips. My first smile from Willow, I will do everything I can to earn more of them while she is in my care.

The sound of her stomach growling echoes throughout the church. My gaze turns sharp as Willow looks away.

"Is there a place I could lie down?"

With only a terse nod, I lead her towards the door behind the altar. There is a short staircase that tapers down to where the former Father used to reside. The air is dank, and I make sure to light the torches along the wall as we pass to scare off any small rodents who have made their homes down here.

The room is in poor shape once we reach it.

The stone doorframe is crumbling—the door hangs from two old iron hinges. Pushing it open, it makes a loud creak before coming to rest against the wall. The bed—more like a cot—has seen better days, but the sheets and pillows are new. I'm glad I had the foresight to use my magic to ready this area before leading Willow down here.

She's been through enough today, watching a gargoyle use magic might just throw her over the edge.

Stepping into the room, she surveys the bare walls. Sitting down on the mattress's edge, it creaks but holds her weight. I linger in the doorway, afraid to leave her but knowing I must. She looks unsure as her gaze finally reconnects with mine.

"I wouldn't mind getting some rest," she says. "Alone. If that's alright."

I nod, but make no moves to leave. Her eyes trail along my body, lingering on my claws and the wings along my back. Under her stare, I feel naked even if I'm dressed in a simple pair of cotton pants.

"Are you going to kill me?"

The question is asked so quietly I barely hear it. My blood freezes into ice as I rear back. Gripping the doorframe to keep from stumbling, I shake my head quickly.

"No. Never."

Willow nods as if mulling over my words. After a moment, her shoulders slump.

"I want to believe you."

My heart seems to stop beating for a moment. Willow laughs softly, but there is no humor in it. Shaking her head, a sad smile dances on her lips.

"Even if you're lying, there's nothing I could do to stop you."

Gliding like a wraith along the stone floors, the edge of her sheet brushes me as she takes the door in her hand. It groans shut on its worn hinges, and the latch catches. I stand there for a moment, unsure what to do with myself. A draft comes and opens the door just a fraction as I hear Willow settle onto the bed.

She's just inside there—on the other side of the door. Hungry, alone, and afraid, I wish I could offer her comfort, and I wish she would accept it. What I desire more than anything is to make her feel safe and cared for.

It all makes sense to me now. I was not awoken from my curse to be her lover—though if she asked me to bed her this instant, I would be unable to resist. No, my purpose in her life is more important than an evening of pleasure. I have been tasked with protecting her. Just as I had watched over monasteries full of Sisters for decades, she is my true purpose—in need of my singular attention and focus.

My fate is to uphold the vow made at my creation. To protect and serve those most vulnerable. She is a Sister who has clearly been neglected by the One True Faith. We have both been harmed by the cruelty masquerading as pious devotion.

The only way we can truly break free of it is together—our

fates woven as one that will lead us to true salvation. My future is tied to the woman lying on the threadbare cot.

I will do everything I can to provide for her, and that starts now. I have a lot of work to do to prove myself a worthy protector.

Dealing with her rumbling stomach will be the perfect place to start.

3

WILLOW

Despite my best efforts, sleep does not find me.

The small cot was comfortable, far more so than any of the beds at Thorncatcher Monastery. The scent of damp wasn't too unpleasant. Even the thin pillow supported my head just fine. My mind was the real issue. It wouldn't stop racing no matter how much my body longed for sleep.

I haven't determined if my new situation is worse than my last. The monastery was not without its stifling rules, presided over by the odious Father Knoll. Here, at least, I am free from that monster, but now faced with one of a different ilk.

For three days, I'll be trapped here with that thing. *No, not a thing,* I silently chastise myself, *Baezal.* He is to be my only companion for the foreseeable future. I should start thinking of him more charitably.

He said he would not hurt me, and I desperately want to believe him.

The only knowledge I have of his kind is what the Faith taught us. It was said they were demons, ones that preyed upon the flesh of virgin Sisters—defiling and devouring them. It was only when the True Blessed Father was able to encase them in stone that we were finally free from their treachery. Their stone bodies were put up in churches as a reminder to all parishioners of the dangers that lurked outside the One True Faith.

To stray from the church was to invite demons into your bed.

However, Baezal did not act like a demon. He's shown me more kindness in the last hour than Sister Grayvle ever has. He gave me a covering and led me down here to sleep. Baezal did not protest when I locked the door, though that flimsy lock would hardly stop him if he wanted to come in here.

He had magic—that was taught to us in the stories, and I tasted metal the moment I came down here. I can only pray he was using it for a benevolent cause.

Still, the simple fact remains that the moment he was freed from his stone prison, he had been kind to me. Baezal had even made vows of protection. That had to mean something. He did not seem bound to this place in any way. If he could escape this church, maybe I could ask him to take me with him.

A wicked thought blooms.

What if I did leave this church with Baezal? What if, in three days' time, Father Knoll returns and I am long gone from here? I would have to forsake the Faith. That idea normally gave me pause in the past. While I had no family to speak of, all I've ever known is life as a Sister. Even if I haven't felt connected to my prayers in years, can I really leave it all behind?

What will I become if I stay here? Father Knoll will surely harm me. It's a miracle I haven't fallen victim to him yet. There are others I am not sure could say the same, and my heart breaks for them.

No, I cannot go back.

I will be brave like the heroes in my books. When I see Baezal again, I will ask him to take me from this place. God willing, he is sympathetic to my plight.

While he may not be the rugged knight I had envisioned as my rescuer, he could very well still be. An odd flush breaks out along my skin when I think of him. He should be repulsive to me. The gray skin and scales—the wings—all parts of his blasphemous form. Yet his face is handsome. The admission steals my breath.

His hair looks as soft as black silk, and my fingers itch to shift through it.

Not to mention the muscles of his chest and stomach. God spare me, he may have been hewn from the marble he was once trapped in. I wonder what those ridges would feel like against my hand, my body, my lips, my—

I let out a groan as a wave of wantonness flames to life within me. I cannot stop it. My desire is always there, brewing under the surface. Having Baezal become the object of its inferno is surprising but not unpleasant. Once my curiosity is piqued about another, my mind runs wild with the fantasy. Though the men in them normally lack a face, this one does.

If I'm being honest, this isn't too shocking a revelation. My favorite story is the one about the rugged knight who has just returned from battle. He finds his way into the tower of the princess to free her. At first, he refuses to remove his helmet— scared she'll find his scarred face ghastly. Instead of recoiling at the gruesome sight, she takes him into her bed and her heart, stating that love is more permanent than any scar.

They would go on to pledge their love to each other and live a quiet life filled with devotion and passion. That is the future I want for myself—it could still be mine if only I can find a way out of here. I must pray that Baezal will help me. I will do anything to not have to return to Thorncatcher Monastery.

With a groan, I flop down onto the bed. Any hope of sleeping evaporates. A scent teases my nose, and my empty stomach growls to life. I haven't had anything to eat since my measly bowl of porridge at breakfast. Rolling off the bed, my feet hit the cold stone floor. I secure my thin covering around myself, and gently push open the door to my room.

Fragrant garlic and onions dance in the air. The scent of roasting meat and fresh bread enlivens my senses. Like a dying man searching for water, I follow the smells down the short corridor. My stomach leads me there, hunger lowering my guard. If Baezal wants to kill me, surely he would allow me one final meal.

Orange light pours over the stone floor at the end of the hall. Once I reach it, I notice a small kitchen back here. It is simple, made up of only a small table with two chairs, a simple metal stove and oven, and a small cabinet filled with all manner of jarred items.

Thick stew boils away atop the stove in a heavy pot. The sight steals my breath as the heavenly aroma overwhelms my senses. The food inside the monastery is only marginally better than gruel. This stew is decadent—sinful—and my mouth waters at the thought of devouring it all.

Glancing at the table, I notice a basket of steaming bread wrapped loosely in a towel. A goblet of wine rests next to a porcelain bowl. I gasp when I see the dress draping along the back of the chair. I approach slowly, my hand feeling over the thick satin material. This is finer than any of my robes. Such fabrics are only for heathens. Though I suppose that's what I've been condemned as, so I might as well take full advantage.

Glancing around to make sure I'm alone, I let my covering drop and fit the gown over my head. It is slightly too big around my chest, but otherwise it fits snugly. The deep blue shade is gorgeous and only a few shades darker than Baezal's eyes.

A fresh wave of heat coats my cheeks, and I have to shake myself. How did all this get here? Surely an abandoned church would not be well stocked with food?

As if in answer, a soft scraping sound echoes from behind me. Turning, I try to keep my face neutral as I find Baezal leaning in the doorway. An ache begins to form inside me. My heart begins to pound—not in fear as it did when I first saw him—but with curiosity.

I swallow thickly, licking my suddenly dry lips.

"You did all this?"

The question seems ridiculous, of course, he did. However, Baezal nods anyway, stepping fully into the room. The flames highlight the impressive plains of his chest. His scales glisten, and my ache deepens. I haven't felt like this before—not without reading one of my books or drowning in a prolonged fantasy. This desire rages inside, focusing squarely on Baezal.

Gesturing towards the stove, the skin of his cheeks darkens.

"You were hungry."

God, is he blushing? I might just faint here and now. No, I must steal myself—I need his help to free me from this place. That is my goal. If he wants me in exchange for his help, that will be no chore at all.

I would lie down with this gargoyle for his help. Hell, I'll bed him out of my own curiosity. I should be repulsed by myself, but I cannot deny it. If I am to break free of the Faith, then leaning into my true nature is the first step.

I'm getting ahead of myself, though. Gargoyles may not even be capable of such things—or he may not desire me in that way. He had called me beautiful, but he could've just been being polite. In my novels, there's always an indication of mutual arousal on the man's part. A secret they cannot keep hidden. Though when I quickly glance down at Baezal's lap, I see no such stirrings that would indicate his desire for me flows as hotly as mine does for him.

Blue flames dance in his gaze as my eyes return to his.

"Eat," he commands in his deep voice.

Goosebumps erupt all over my skin. I'd gladly listen to any command he gave me. There would be no need for rebellion if he were the one keeping me. The other Sisters were right, I must be cursed with a wanton soul. How else would you describe it?

All my previous fantasies of lovers have shifted. Now, all I see are gray scales and piercing blue eyes. Fangs and claws, and hair glossier than silk. My hands tremble as I grip my bowl and carefully ladle soup into it.

Heavy steam rises from the thick broth. Bits of root vegetables and beef float to the surface. I blow on a spoonful before greedily sucking it down. It's good—divine. My stomach sings its appreciation as I eat bits of vegetables and meat. My eyes glance up to find Baezal watching me carefully from the doorway.

His eyes betray nothing, but his chest rises and falls in quick succession. Setting down my spoon, I gesture towards the chair across from me.

"Won't you join me?"

Baezal seems to weigh my words. Finally, he clicks over to me, his large wings fitting over the back of the chair and flexing in front of the roaring fireplace. The chair groans as his massive frame settles atop it. Even his arms are impressive, thickly coiled with muscle and wider than my thighs.

My thighs—which are now turning slick with arousal—clench together. The heavy silence stretches as I tuck back into my meal. Baezal watches me as I devour the whole bowl. Once it is empty, his posture seems to relax.

"Where did you get all this?" I ask, reaching for a piece of warm bread.

Popping it onto my tongue, it melts in my mouth. I groan, quickly reaching for another. Baezal's eyes track my every movement.

"Village," he says as I ingest another piece of bread.

I raise an eyebrow.

"You stole it?"

Baezal shrugs, and I cannot even be mad. Stealing is a part

of this new world I find myself in. I'm glad he had done it because if it were up to me, I'm not sure I would've been brave enough.

If he can freely go to the village to procure me food and clothing, then surely he can take me from this place. He has to know of some safe place, somewhere I can find employment and earn a wage. I have some skills from being a Sister that are surely needed in a small village.

Gripping my goblet, I take a sip of the red wine for courage. I have to make an ally of him sooner rather than later. This is my first chance to do that. The bitter liquid loosens my tongue as I train my gaze on Baezal's.

"How did you become trapped here?"

His eyes flare to life as his dark brows pull low.

"Cursed," he snarls.

A male of few words, cannot say I'm surprised. Silence settles in as I take another sip of wine. Perhaps that was too forward a question to start out with. Before I can try again, Baezal tears off another piece of bread and hands it to me. My heart begins to race as a flush erupts all over my body.

I take it with shaking hands. My fingers graze his, and I have to swallow my moan. I've been starved of another's touch —my desire for it is making me lose sense of what's most important. My freedom.

"How did you come to be here?" he asks.

I take a bite of bread, chewing and swallowing before deciding how to answer. There is no point in lying to him. If I want to gain his trust, then unfiltered honesty will surely be the best way to do that. Taking a sip of wine, I lean against the wooden back of my chair.

"Got in trouble. I was discovered kissing a local boy. Father Knoll was not pleased by my actions."

Baezal hums a low growl in his throat. Taking another sip of wine, I press on.

"Before I knew it, I was loaded into a carriage and left here to contemplate my sins." The wine has done its job, as I am powerless to stop the words slipping from my lips. "Secretly, I believe Father Knoll's true irritation is the fact that someone other than him touched me. Vile man. He's been planning something for me—I know it. Therefore, I cannot say that I'm too upset at being here and away from him. Away from all of them."

Baezal's eyes give nothing away. He watches me carefully, and I worry, as the silence stretches, that I've said too much. I hold my breath, only letting it out once he gives me a simple nod. Hope pumps thickly through my veins.

If anyone was to understand my plight, it would be Baezal. Reaching for the final piece of bread, I chew it slowly, summoning my strength to ask my next question.

"Baezal," I say carefully, watching his eyes blaze. "I was wondering—well, hoping really—if you could help me escape this place."

His wings pull tight behind him, the motion causing a swift breeze to disrupt my hair. The scent of crackling wood from the fire turns heavy. His claws curl along the worn table top, gently scraping the surface.

"Where do you wish to go?"

"Anywhere that isn't here."

My reply is instant and true. I do not give much care where I end up. Perhaps a place near water, where I can finally see the bright blue sea I've read about. Yes, I would like that very much.

Shaking free of my childish fantasy, I lean forward.

"I want to leave the True Faith behind," I confess. "My only request is that you take me somewhere they won't find me. Somewhere I can break free from my obligations and live as I've always wanted—unburdened."

Silence fills the room, save for the crackling hearth. Baezal looks at me, and a flurry of emotions crowds his glorious eyes.

Something sparks in his irises as if seeing me for the very first time. What must he think of me? A Sister—remanded for her transgression and begging for his help to leave the True Faith behind.

All my prayers and teachings seem hollow. A sharp pain pierces my heart as I realize I never meant any of them. My vows to the Sisterhood were given, not out of devotion but of expectation. I was forced into this role, and that is why my soul is restless. A pious life was never mine to lead.

From this moment on, I will live for myself—taking what I want and doing exactly as my heart commands me. I am no longer owned by the One True Faith. Their rules no longer bind me. The shame once inflicted on me dissipates—who are they to judge me?

Sister Willow is dead—it is only Willow now.

She will be a fearsome thing to behold once fully unleashed.

"I will help you." Baezal nods thoughtfully. "It will take some time for me to prepare for our journey, but I know just a place to take you. Somewhere they'll never go looking. I make this vow to you."

Elation races through me, making my pulse pound. A smile stretches my lips until my cheeks ache. Baezal's cheeks darken, and he looks away towards the fire.

Freedom is within reach. He will help me—take me some-place where I can start my life over. This is what I dreamed of. So what if my knight happens to have scales and wings? He saved me nonetheless. Baezal is just as valiant as any scarred hero.

Without thinking, I take his hand in mine. His eyes fly towards mine, widening. His palm nearly covers my entire hand. Clasping it between both my palms, I bring it towards my chest. My heart pounds against his rough skin. Baezal sucks in a breath as he stares at our joined hands.

Pale, fleshy pink surrounding rough, scaly gray is quite the sight to behold.

"Thank you," I whisper.

Baezal shivers at my words, his hand tightening against mine ever so slightly. A delicious thrill runs through me as I survey him. His hand could easily snap me in half, yet it holds mine so gently. His massive frame could crush me. Still, every touch has been featherlight. Veins protrude from the thick column of his neck before giving way into the deadly cut of his jaw. Inky black hair falls over his shoulder, and my fingers itch to touch it.

I meant what I said to him. The True Faith's teachings no longer apply to me. With this new chance at freedom, I leave behind all the vows I once took. I swore to be pious and humble—to be unwavering in my devotion—and above all else to remain pure and chaste.

Chastity is the first tenet I wish to disavow.

I stare at Baezal and consider my next move. He's been nothing but kind to me, and now that he's offered to help me, I want to thank him in a way that shows him just how grateful I am. However, more than that, I want to be free—to experience the pleasures I've read about for years. Ultimately, I want the chance to choose someone of my own volition.

And I'm choosing Baezal.

Carefully, I lower his hand back to the table. Sadness tinges his gaze, and I have to swallow my giggle. He will not be bereft of my touch too much longer. Clutching my wine goblet, I drink down the remaining liquid so as not to lose my nerve.

He may very well reject me—this is all a bit sudden, I can admit that. Yet, it feels right. My heart has chosen him—my savior and protector. He is who I want to be with for my first time. I've felt more at the brush of his hand than I ever have with another.

My soul is leading me towards him, and I'd be a fool to ignore its urging.

I lick my lower lip and allow my hair to slip over one shoulder. Trailing my finger along the table, I capture his blue gaze once more.

"Baezel," I sigh softly, nearly purring at his shiver. "I must confess something to you. Won't you hear it?"

"Yes."

His growl echoes around the room, and the skin between my thighs grows even damper. The pulsing ache has returned with a frenzy, demanding to be satisfied.

"The other Sisters believed me cursed—said I had the soul of a demon."

Baezal rears back, eyes large in his gray face.

"Impossible."

A small smile curves my lips.

"Normally, I would agree with you, but I fear they may have been right. You see, there's always been this wickedness inside of me." My fingers skim up the side of his palms, his scales rising to meet my wandering hand. "I was always getting in trouble with the Elder Sisters—reprimanded for my desires. Father Knoll said intense prayer was my only chance at salvation, though it did very little to stop my hedonist thoughts."

My fingers trail up his forearm, nails biting into the hard, rigid of muscle. Baezal's powerful chest rises and falls. Full, gray lips part to reveal the fangs lurking inside his mouth. What would his bite feel like? I will not be satisfied until I discover it.

"At first, my wickedness blossomed innocently. Sneaking off during prayer time or staying up past curfew. Then there were the books. The Elder Sisters would've killed me had they discovered what I was consuming. Do you want to know what was written on these sinful pages?"

Baezal swallows, his nod is swift as my fingers draw swirls along his scales.

"They were tales of battles—heroes earning glory. However, they were mostly tales of love—beddings of fair maidens by their handsome knights under the pale moonlight. Those books inflamed what lay dormant within me. A wantonness the True Faith was determined to see snuffed out."

Licking my lips, I watch Baezal's claws embed themselves in the table. Splinters rise around his strong fingers, but he pays them no mind.

"My wicked soul made me seek out local boys and share kisses with them in stolen moments."

My heart races as heat spreads along my body. I hardly recognize my own voice. This is the real me—the one who is open about her wants. A seductress that's been stifled for far too long.

Lifting my hand not touching Baezal, I reach for the sleeve of my gown.

"It made me touch myself beneath the covers at night—swallowing down my moans as I imagined myself being ravaged just like the women I had read about."

Yanking down the sleeve of my gown, the swells of my breasts come into view. The movement nearly bears them entirely. My nipples are barely concealed by the lace neckline.

Rising on shaking knees, I pull my hand from him and pad slowly along the floor.

"Do you understand now, Baezal? If I am truly to break free of the True Faith, then I must give myself to someone. To experience the one thing I've wanted for as long as I can remember."

Baezal's eyes are wholly black as I approach him in the chair. Even seated, we are eye level with each other. The skirt of my gown brushes his splayed thighs. I bite my lip to keep from grinning at the hardness tenting the front of his pants. My earlier doubts are elevated—he wants me just as much.

He hands curl onto his knees—in an effort to keep from grabbing me, I hope.

"Willow, you—you don't have to give yourself to me. I will help you regardless."

Disappointment threatens to weaken my resolve. If my books have taught me anything, it's that glory only belongs to the brave.

"Does that mean you don't want me?" I ask.

Baezal rears back as if he's been struck.

"Of course, I want you. From the moment I was freed from my stone prison, my thoughts have been filled only by your face, your scent. My desire for you is not why I protest."

Pleasure skims soft fingertips down my spine. Goosebumps erupt all over my flesh in delight. I move closer towards him, sliding fully between his legs. My hands fall to his strong shoulders, and with a snarl, his hands find their home on my waist.

Nothing has ever felt more perfect than this.

"I've always been curious, but I've never been intrigued by something so completely as I am now." My breasts nearly graze his chin as he looks up at me. "Shall I tell you what that is?"

"Please," he snarls.

His claws press into my waist, the sharp pricks pressing through the fabric. With a smile, I rise up and claim a seat on his lap. The chair beneath us groans as I position myself. His seeking hardness rests against my wet flesh. Baezal hiss as my hands skim up his shoulders to tangle in his hair.

Softer than silk and hotter than fire, the dark strands shift between my fingers.

"Since the moment I entered this room, I've wondered what you taste like."

With my heady confession still ringing in both our ears, I lean forward. My breasts pillow against his chest, and my eyes flutter shut. My lips meet his firm ones in a hard press. The touch is slight—the kiss is beyond chaste. The skirt of my gown hikes up around my hips.

Baezal's loud groan vibrates his chest. The sound unlocks something within my heart—a deep well that's been suppressed for years. It's been unleashed now, and with it, a potent desire rushes through my veins.

I know, without a shadow of doubt, that nothing from this moment on will ever be the same.

4

BAEZAL

The first brush of her lips against mine renders me immobile.

I'm not sure what I'm meant to do. It is as if I'm a spectator looking down at the two of us from above. I see my stiff posture as this beautiful, wanton creature crawls into my lap. The neckline of her dress nearly bares her entire chest. Her skirts tuck up around her waist, exposing her smooth, pale calves.

Delicate hands burrow into my hair and hold me firm as she presses her supple lips against my own. My hands tremble along her waist. I'm scared to move—to even breathe too deeply—and break whatever spell is at work here. Surely it is magic, or at the very least a miracle, to have this angel in my lap. To feel the heat seeping from her core and teasing my raging cock to a painful state.

She gasps against me, the sound as sweet as she tastes. The touch of our lips is featherlight, and yet it unmakes me on the spot. I want to snarl and haul her against me. My fingers itch to shred the satin of her gown until she is naked and trembling before me. I want to lay claim to her for all the world to see—to know she is mine in every way. My primal urges reach a new peak as her lips shift against me once more, satisfaction humming in her throat.

My fingers dig into her waist, urging her closer as she continues our chaste kiss. I have to take care with my urges and not scare this wonderful, beautiful little human who's crawled into my lap. Who's mere presence nearly drives me to madness. Her breathy confessions of her sin had nearly made me spill in my pants.

Willow is unlike any Sister I've come across. Throughout my time serving the One True Faith, I had, of course, come across unhappy Sisters. Ones that would leave the True Faith never to be seen again. There is more than unhappiness in Willow's plight. She is a bird trapped in a pious cage, forced to be something that is in direct contrast with her soul.

Desire burns brightly within her—I can taste it on her lips, feel it in the way she touches me.

That is why I must take care of her. Life as a Sister is pious —removed from the world at large, they are forged into innocent vessels who know only what the True Faith teaches them. They are taught very little of love and absolutely nothing of lust. For someone like Willow, it would be very easy to conflate the two.

She may desire me, as ridiculous as it sounds, but she doesn't want me. Not at least in the way she believes she does. I am not a hero from her storybooks; I am a monster. One who will worship her for as long as I am allowed. I will give her pleasure and show her the heights her body can reach. Then she will learn to revel in another's embrace—seek out the man she truly loves and begin her life with him once I free her.

That is the only future I can foresee.

Even the notion of her touching another like this makes red mist over my vision. My chest tightens, and I greedily suck down lungfuls of her lavender scent. My wings pull tight behind me, flapping sharply in agitation. Willow is blissfully unaware of my agony. She merely presses her lips more firmly against mine, nestling as close as she can.

Her dark lashes fan out atop her pink cheeks. Each shift of her hips brings my seed dangerously close to spilling. It's been a century since I last touched another like this. None of those who shared a bed with me in the past made me feel like Willow does. My madness for her only worsens the longer she touches me. It will be a miracle if I can make it through this night with an ounce of my sanity still intact.

Small hands tug at my hair, and I meet her kiss with one of my own. Our lips dance together, remaining closed. My claws press harder into her sides, and she shivers. This fabric is barely a barrier, yet it must remain in place for now. She is the one who determines our pace and how much she wants from me.

With a sigh, Willow pulls back. Her chest rises and falls rapidly behind the top of her gown. What I wouldn't give to taste one of her hard nipples. They are there, locked in their satin prison, begging me to free them. My hands remain still, even as Willow lowers her forehead to mine. Her deep brown eyes are brilliant, highlighted by the flush of her cheeks.

"I didn't expect this," she confesses. "Didn't expect you to…"

Wickedness kindles in her gaze as her pink tongue sneaks out from between her lips. Shifting slightly, her tongue glides slowly against my jaw. My claws embed themselves in her sides, feeling her warm flesh. My groan echoes around the room, rattling her discarded bowl and goblet.

"Taste so good," she finishes. "This is the best kiss I've ever had."

She licks her lips for good measure, and my restraint hangs on by a thread. I haul her closer. Her lithe thighs stretch around my waist. The scent of her arousal chokes me. I can feel her soaking the front of my pants. One quick tug and I would be deep inside her tight, wet heat.

"Do you want more?" I ask, my voice sounding not like my own.

Willow's eyes brighten as she nods eagerly.

"Please." Her lips press against my jaw where her tongue just was. "Everywhere."

Her wickedness teases my own. Primal possession surges within me. A satisfied grin spreads across my face. The heat in my blood loosens my tongue.

"You would've wasted away inside that monastery," I decree. "A woman as wanton and passionate as you should've had your desires satisfied long ago by an eager servant."

She hums deep in her throat, her lips falling against mine, but I hold back. Looking into her eyes, I let her glimpse my madness—at what her slight touches have turned me into.

"I will become your most ardent worshipper. Even if it is only for tonight, I will kindle the flames of your lust and give you the pleasures you so desperately seek."

"Please, Baezal. Kiss me again."

Satisfaction spreads throughout me. Her words about my prowess when it comes to the other males who have kissed her please me. I can only hope that with each touch I bestow on her, the memory of their touches will fade into nothing.

"Here?" I ask, brushing my lips against her throat.

Willow's head falls back, and the long dark tendrils of her hair brush my hands on her waist. I lick over her pounding pulse. My teeth graze her tender flesh and delight in her whimper. My exploration is slow, measured. I will savor her tonight knowing that our time together is fleeting.

Lavender dances on my tongue as I lick behind her ear. Her breasts rub against my hard chest as I nibble her earlobe. A voice whispers at me to bite her—mark her as mine—but I manage to resist it. My lips trail down her throat again, loving the way she holds me close to her.

Beautiful and trusting, Willow is beyond my wildest dreams.

My teeth graze the column of her pale neck. Her arousal swirls around us and makes my mouth water. For a moment, my control slips, and my teeth press down. Not hard enough to break the skin, but enough to make her gasp. Her eyes fly open —black pupils nearly devouring her entire iris.

"More," she demands.

I nip at her again, delighting in the shudder that runs through her. My claws skim up her sides, tickling as I go. They linger at the top of her gown, shaking with the need to pull it off her, but I hold off. I must go slow, for both our sakes.

"Would you like a kiss here?" I ask, tongue skimming along her collarbone.

My chest rests against the fleshy swell of her breasts as I taste her soft skin. Willow's fingers tighten on my head, holding me closer to her chest as I lick and suck my way across. Her moans are soft, pleading with me to keep going.

"Baezal," she sighs. "I need more. Touch me everywhere. Don't stop—I've never felt like this before. Never wanted another as much as I want you."

If my ego had been satisfied before, I am fairly certain I am floating. This glorious angel wants me—even if it is only for tonight, and she will realize the error of her desire soon enough. Her declaration pleases me. I will take care of her, knowing that her lust for me is misplaced. She would've felt this way about anyone who rescued her. I am sure of it. Still, I will be grateful for even the chance to touch her. It's more than a monster like me deserves.

My lips find her throat, licking into the hollow.

"You are a goddess," I murmur against her skin. "Bestowing this kindness on a wretch like me, I'll honor your sacrifice. The

True Faith sought to cage you. Tonight I will help free you. I will stoke your passion until you find the one you truly desire."

Lust and devotion thrum through me. The candor of my words barely registers until Willow stiffens in my arms. I play back what I just said and curse myself for being such a simpering fool. Glancing up, all pleasure is gone from her face. Her dark eyes are hard as they stare down at me.

I want to bash my head against the nearest wall. Why did I have to say anything? She's clearly coming to her senses now and sees me for who I truly am. The monster she was about to debase herself with—she will be repulsed by me. I don't know if I will be able to withstand her rejection.

I'd rather be cursed into stone a thousand times over than lose her touch.

However, that is exactly what happens, as Willow gathers her skirts and slides off of me. The loss of her warmth is a physical blow, nearly sending me to the floor. The scent of her pleasure is retreating. The roaring fire paints her lovely face in deep shadows.

"What you say is blasphemous." Willow swallows thickly, before shaking her head. "But it is also untrue. I am not a goddess—merely a woman of twenty-one who knows very little of the world beyond the walls of the monastery. There is, however, one thing I know. One thing not even Father Knoll or Sister Grayvle could take from me, and that was what I know of *myself*."

The final world is thrown between us on the floor. Determination blazes in her eyes. Crossing her arms over her chest, she straightens her spine.

"I did not kiss you out of gratitude—even though I am grateful for your help. I did not do so out of pity or because I wanted experience before settling down with a human lover. I did it because I wanted *you*."

Her words leave me too stunned to speak, so I merely watch

her fierceness grow into a raging fire. This may be her most lovely form.

"For the first time in my life, I had the chance to seize the thing I wanted without fear of consequences or judgment. It may seem sudden, but this is what I truly want. You are what I want. We could part ways tomorrow, and I'd hold tonight in my heart until my death."

The flames of the fire burn low as silence settles in between us. I don't know what to say to her. I can hardly believe her words, yet there is no trace of deception. She wants me, as I am. Not because I am her rescuer or the first creature she's been free to explore. She desires me simply for being myself. I need to make amends for my foolish behavior.

Swiftly.

"Willow," I say softly, rising from the chair. "I am sorry. It is my own past that made me doubt you."

She has offered me so much of herself, trusted me beyond what I deserve. It is only fair that I lay bare my soul to her. These memories are unpleasant, but there can be no space for lies between us. More than that, I want to share my past with Willow in hopes that, in doing so,our future has the chance to flourish.

"Long ago, before I was cursed, there was a Sister in the monastery I was tasked with watching over. I'm not sure what your histories teach now, but my kind were created to protect the One True Faith as guardians over the Sisters who inhabited the halls. Sister Kylne was a pretty young woman with fiery red hair. She had a tendency for accidents, so I tasked myself with keeping her from any accidents in the courtyard when she stumbled on the way to prayer."

Willow's brows pull low, but she remains silent.

"I dreamed the smiles she gave me and the accidental brushes of her hand against mine meant something. I had a fondness for her that I believed was being reciprocated until one night. I kissed her." Shaking my head, I run a hand down my face. "Or at least I tried to. She screamed as I got too close. Her repulsion was evident, especially as she condemned me as the other Sisters gathered. Sickened by the idea that a monster like me would seek to desecrate her purity."

"Baezal," Willow breathes.

"I was cast out after that. Adrift for a few years in different towns until I found refuge here. I hadn't known at the time that my situation was about to become bleaker. The True Blessed Father discovered me and transformed me into stone. I never thought I'd wake from my curse—I'd nearly given up hope."

My eyes connect with hers, and I take a small step forward.

"You are special to me, Willow. My savior—the one who freed me from my curse. I couldn't live with myself if you came to regret anything that happened between us. Don't you see now why I couldn't believe your desire to be real?"

Reaching out slowly, I cup her petal-soft cheek. She doesn't push me away. If anything, she leans into my touch.

"I've glimpsed your soul, Willow. It is just as beautiful as you are. We may have only just met, but I know you—I see you. Kind, compassionate, brave, even if you know little of this world, you are already the best part of it."

Willow blinks up at me several times with shining eyes. Moisture beads along her lower lashes, but no tears fall. Color dances on her round cheeks.

"Can you ever forgive me?" I ask.

I hold my breath as a flurry of emotions kindles in her gaze. The light burns low around us. Rain echoes in from outside. Willow's full lips pull into a wanton grin. I let loose a breath frozen in my lungs.

"There's a better way you can apologize to me," she says. "It still involves your mouth. Just fewer words."

Taking my hand, she tugs me closer to her. In one swift movement, she slides the sleeves of her dress down and allows the garment to fall from her body. She stands before me naked, glowing like an angel in the firelight. Her nudity is different than when I first saw her. She is allowing me this unencumbered view because she wants me to see her.

I'm not sure where to look first. Even her toes are enticing to me. Dark pink nipples stand at attention, begging for my mouth. Beneath a thatch of dark hair is her glistening flesh. Arousal decorates her delicate inner thighs. The scent of her desire is heady.

Willow smiles up at me as she slowly guides my hand to her breast. I squeeze it gently, my scales rising with pleasure. My wings feel heavy, and my breath turns uneven.

"Kiss me here," she commands.

I drop to my knees, my head at the perfect level with her breasts. I lick her exposed nipple, gently rolling it with my tongue. Willow moans, swaying on her feet. My other hand wraps around her waist to keep her steady. I stare up at her and suck her nipple deeper into my mouth. Her pupils are blown wide with pleasure. Lavender coats every one of my senses.

Lifting our joined hands, she trails them down her soft stomach and through the small dusting of hair. I hiss as she presses my palm against her wet pussy. She is soft and dripping into my hand.

"And most importantly here."

I give her a gentle squeeze and watch her eyes roll back in her head. She leaves my hand resting between her thighs and places her palms on my shoulders. They squeeze me tightly as my tongue licks a path towards her other breasts to show it equal attention. She tastes sweeter than honey.

In my grip, I lightly tease her wet entrance. Barely sliding a finger past her opening, her tightness makes my mouth go dry. Willow's thighs flex around my hand, rocking back and forth, desperate for any type of friction. My angel needs a climax. She's desperate for one.

I have rudimentary knowledge of how to please a woman. Unlike the Sisters of the True Faith, I never took any vows of chastity. Still, my limited experience is with the human women I had to pay handsomely to ignore my monstrous form. They seemed to enjoy themselves, but that's what my gold paid for.

This is uncharted territory for me, but luckily, Willow's body is more than responsive. Whatever she enjoys the most, I have no doubt I'll be able to tell.

Parting her slit, my fingers find her clit. A simple graze of my claw against it makes Willow's mouth part on a scream. A good indication. I tease her nipple with my teeth, biting gently as Willow begins to pant. She thrust herself against my palm. I rub her clit harder, delighting in her whimpers of pleasure.

"Feels so good," she sighs. "No one has ever touched me there. Only you."

I smile against her breast, loving the sound of that. My fingers alternate between rubbing her clit and testing her entrance. Licking a path between her breasts, I capture her chin in my other hand and pull her eyes towards mine.

"Did you save yourself for me? Kept this pussy tight and untouched all these years because you knew it would please me?"

Her nod is jerky.

"Y—yes," she babbles. "Even when I didn't know you existed. I could've chosen another—been disavowed by the True Faith for doing so, but I didn't. I never knew why. Not until now. I was waiting for you."

"Good girl," I snarl, nipping at the side of her breast.

"I endured it all, and in the end, every choice I made led me here. To you." Her hands sink into my hair and cradle my skull. "It's fate."

Fate. How can one simple word hold so much meaning? Willow is my fate. She is what broke the curse.

In the face of your fate, you will reawaken.

It is not merely as a protector as I once thought, but as her lover as well. The male who safeguards her heart and brings her pleasure. I can be both—I want to be both.

Willow has already claimed my heart and soul. I will prove myself worthy in time to earn hers. Tonight, I will show her exactly what our future could be if she allows me to keep her. The pleasures I can offer her will be far beyond those any human man could give. She's given me the chance to show her all I can give. I will not squander the opportunity.

I let go of her breasts with a pop. Her eyes fly to mine. Willow's lips part as my nose glides down the center of her body. Reaching the apex of her thighs, I press a firm kiss atop the dark hair covering her pussy. Hooking my hands around her waist, she gives a squeak of surprise as I lift her from the stone floor.

Nodding my head, the small table is quickly cleared of any remaining dishes. I set her down atop the scratched surface. Her legs hang limply off the sides. Red and pink paint over her cheeks and chest. Even her knees are highlighted in scarlet. Her breathing is ragged as her arms rest loosely at her sides. She makes no move to cover herself, and I hum with satisfaction.

Staring down at my delicious feast, I say a prayer of thanks to whatever gods may be out there.

"Are you going to come on my tongue, my angel?"

Dark eyes turn glossy. Her dark hair fans out behind her like a veil. A soft breath hitches in her throat as she nods. With a grin, I collapse atop her body. My lips find her in a searing kiss. Licking the seam of her mouth, she parts it tentatively. My innocent angel did not know tongues could be used during kissing, it would seem.

Hers is timid as it brushes against mine. It only takes a few moments of coaxing before it begins fighting mine for dominance. We are soon in a battle of teeth and lashing tongues. I drink down her moans like wine as she thrusts herself against me. Her short nails tease the base of my wings. They spread over us, cocooning us in a nest of passion.

Raising my knee between her legs, her hot center quickly finds it. She thrusts herself against me, dampening the fabric of my pants with her sweet arousal as incoherent moans slip from her lips. I kiss along her jaw. Nuzzling into her ear, my teeth tug at her lobe.

"Will you let me tongue fuck your virgin cunt, sweet Willow?"

She gasps at my crude words, her eyes going wide. Her wicked soul flames to life as she nods, biting her lip to keep from screaming. I press my knee harder against her, capturing her delicate jaw in my hand.

"You confessed to touching yourself beneath the covers, but that's all you've ever done. Too scared to put even one finger inside yourself, isn't that right? Tell me," I command.

"Yes."

I chuckle against her ear, licking the shell of it. I've been replaced by a feral beast, one who savors each one of her wanton confessions and wishes to test the limits of her wickedness.

"Afraid that if you experienced too much pleasure, you couldn't withstand going without it," I surmise.

"I was scared," she admits. "But not anymore."

"Good girl, angel." I kiss her cheek before returning to her mouth. "Tonight, I'll give you my fingers and tongue. When you are ready, I'll put my cock so deep inside you that you won't be able to walk without feeling me. My seed will drip from your little, pink hole for hours after I've finished with you."

Red spreads across her chest. Her hips grind her more

forcefully against my knee. Her breath catches in her throat as her lavender scent deepens.

"Isn't that what you want? Tell me."

She nods, her head smacking against the table. I tsk at her, retreating my knee just slightly. She gasps, trying to slide down to capture her pleasure, but I hold her steady.

"Use your words, angel."

Her eyes are fevered. Sweat beads along her brow, causing strands of her hair to stick to it. Her lips are red and swollen from my kisses. Willow looks thoroughly ravaged, and we've barely even begun.

"I want you to fuck me with your fingers and tongue."

Before I can be pleased with her confession, wickedness gleams in her eyes. Her hand trails down my chest, past the waistband, until her warm palm cradles my hard cock. Seed leaks from the tip, soaking the front of them. She squeezes me gently, and I nearly come right then.

Biting her lip, Willow is the picture of innocent curiosity.

"Can I suck your cock before you put it inside me, Baezal?"

A roaring echoes through my ears. My blood boils inside my veins.

"Naughty angel," I chastise without heat.

Willow squeezes me again, but I slip out of her grasp. Kissing down her body, I lick over each nipple, causing her to moan. My tongue licks a trail from between her breasts towards her navel. I swirl around it before kissing across her hip bones. Willow moans, her back arching off the table.

Hooking my hands below her knees, I heft both of her legs over my shoulders. Her feet graze the tops of my wings, causing pleasure to skim down my spine. Hoisting her up, I get my first real look at her most intimate flesh. She is pink and perfect, glistening before my gaze. I stare up at her and make sure she's watching as I lower my mouth to her center.

Sweet arousal floods my mouth as I spear my tongue into

her tight hole. I lick deep, skimming along her inner walls. Willow screams, arching clean off the table. Her thighs squeeze my head as I continue to feast from her. My nose nuzzles against her clit. Her blunt nails dig into the table to hold herself steady.

"Sweeter than honey. Tighter than a fist. Perfect."

Each compliment is whispered against her cunt. I taste her fully from top to bottom. Willow screams as my tongue presses against her back entrance. I swirl it around the tight ring of my muscles, my claws biting into the globes of her ass.

"Another time," I vow, returning to her pussy.

"Baezal," she whimpers.

My tongue curls in and out of her. With each thrust, her pussy begins to quiver, tightening around my flexing muscle. Pulling my tongue free, I quickly suck two fingers into my mouth, coating them in saliva. Swirling one into her opening, I tuck the digit just inside. Willow groans, her breathing becoming choppy.

"It's for the best no man ever sampled your pussy, sweet Willow." My tongue drags along her clit as she clenches down on my finger. "A pussy like this deserves battles fought over it— males would forsake God just for one taste of it."

"Baezal!" she screams as I thrust a second finger inside of her.

I'm careful not to go too deep. Her virginity will be broken by my cock. I curl my fingers inside her, scissoring them in a way that leaves her panting. She is close, I can feel it in how her sweet cunt grips my fingers. Her wetness aids their movements. Sloppy, wet sounds echo around us in the small kitchen.

"I am no better than they are. This table is your altar, and my tongue is my prayer. Allow me to show you my unwavering devotion, goddess."

Lowering my lips to her clit, I suck it deep into my mouth. Rolling it with my tongue, I lick it over and over. Her hips begin to canter, and her knuckles turn white where she's gripping the table. Thrusting my fingers deep, I nip at her clit.

"Come."

Willow erupts at my command. My fingers are nearly broken from the force of her climax. Clenching down on me, I continue to suck her clit as her come soaks my face in a flurry of wet splashes. My mouth and hand are drenched in her sweetness. Her screams are hoarse as she shouts my name. Every muscle in her body is rigid.

Once she slumps back to the table, I catch her eye as I pull my fingers from her sheath. I suck them deep into my mouth, savoring her deliciousness. Willow hums in her throat. Dark pupils devour her brown eyes. Satisfaction is written in every line of her body. Giving her one final lick, I prowl up her trembling body.

Aftershocks of pleasure rack her as I take her lips again. I share her taste with her, and she sighs. Her hand cups my face as our tongues twine together. My heart pounds against my ribs in rhythm with hers. We stare at each other for a moment, a thousand different emotions playing across our faces.

My heart reaches for hers. Whether she knows it or not, it belongs to her. In this moment, I can feel the edges of her soul reaching towards mine. We will be joined together soon enough. I just have to be patient. My hand trails along her jaw.

"How do you feel?"

I thumb her full bottom lip, noting her heavy eyelids.

"Alive."

I chuckle, letting my hand fall to the side. Willow slides her legs apart before wrapping them around my waist. Her arms snake around my neck. Pressing her body against mine, she places a soft kiss on my lips.

"Take me to bed," she commands.

Like any good servant, I obey immediately. Hefting her into my arms, I walk her slowly into the chambers she inhabited earlier. Settling us both atop the thin cot, I curl her into my chest and cover us with a blanket. Willow doesn't say another word as she snuggles back against me.

With the taste of her still faintly on my tongue, I know without any doubt that I'd endure a millennium trapped in stone if it led me to having her in my arms just like this.

WILLOW

When I had told Baezal to take me to bed, I hadn't meant for rest.

Yet, that seems to be exactly what happened as my head hit the soft pillow and his warm body had settled in beside me. Now, as I blink open my eyes in the dim room, my body feels rejuvenated. Dozens of taper candles have been lit, casting the room in a warm glow.

Baezal's arm is draped along my waist, and I can feel his strong chest against my back. The memories of what we've shared together this evening come flooding back. I do not regret any of it—quite the opposite. I long for more and hope he isn't resting too deeply so that he cannot be roused for another round.

This was all moving fairly quickly. I'm sure plenty would call me a fool for allowing this to transpire the way it has, but those people are wrong. Baezal and I have not spent much time together, yet I feel as though I know him better than anyone. He has seen me in a way no one else has—cared for me as if it were his sole purpose in life.

Our time together has been short, but precious nonetheless. I know in my heart what we have is true. It is my heart that led me to him, as if it had been searching for his all this time. Now, as I feel it pounding against my shoulder, I feel complete.

My soul itches to be entwined with his.

In one of my stolen novels, I had read about this exact situation. The knight had come to rescue the princess, locked away for years in a tower by her evil father, the king. The moment the knight removed his helmet, and she saw his beautiful scarred face, she knew it was true love. It was a reckless declaration, but no less true.

Is Baezal not the same for me? He is made of scales, claws, and wings instead of scars, but I recognize him just as the princess had her knight. Just as she did, I did not need months of courtship to reach the conclusion my heart had already come to.

The knight, for his part, had fallen instantly in love with the princess and confessed to it before bedding her for the first time. That was how all the best love stories went. While I was certain of my own feelings, I could not be sure of Baezal's.

He had called me a goddess, said he would worship me devoutly, but was that the same as love? The demons in his past could make him wary of trusting me. They had already set our first hurdle. He had been heartbroken before. The pain of that other Sister's rejection made him unworthy of love.

Maybe he just needs more time for me to prove her wrong. I already love him. I can be patient and wait for him to love me back. My future is now one of endless possibilities.

I may not know much of the world, but I know myself. What I had told Baezal had been true. The One True Faith tried to keep me caged. For years, I was forced to repress who I truly was. Even still, I knew what love was—real love. Not the forced devotion they thrust upon us.

I had read about it for years, glimpsed it on our rare trips into the neighboring town.

Baezal's kisses felt different from all the other males because I love him. The local men would've helped me escape from the monastery, but I never asked them. I knew it was because, had I done so, they would expect something in return for their help. A wife at the very least.

I know that Baezal would have helped me if I offered him nothing in return. He'll never seek to cage me. All he's done since the moment we met is provide for me. How could I not love him?

Maybe I am a fool, but love makes fools of us all.

Baezal was meant to save me—even if I didn't understand it at first, I was meant to come here. To awaken him from his curse was my fate, and his is to be my lover and protector. He is my present and my future all in one.

I've spent years being denied what I truly want, and I won't waste another second without claiming my heart's desire.

Claws skim along my sides, tickling just under my ribs. Goosebumps erupt on my naked flesh. Baezal's warm breath tickles my neck. Sighing deeply, I roll onto my other side. I fall into the valley of his chest and stare up into his handsome face.

I had been wrong to fear him when we first met. There is more kindness in his gaze now than ever bestowed on me by anyone in the True Faith.

Tracing the planes of his face with my finger, his wings spread out beside us.

"How long have I been asleep?"

Baezal captures my hand and presses a kiss to my palm.

"Only a few hours. It's still dark outside."

"Good," I sigh.

Baezal raises a brow, but I merely shrug.

"I would've hated to have slept through our first night

together." My eyes fall to his lips, desperate for another taste. "Especially when there's still so much left to explore."

Baezal groans as my hand skims down his chest. The thick ridges of his body are covered in delicate scales. They flex against my fingers. The rough texture of his skin inflames my lust. He is not human—that's part of the reason I desire him so much. He dominates me everywhere. His power is palpable, and yet he is so gentle with me. The juxtaposition of the two reawakens my earlier simmering desire.

There's a small part of me that whispers to be cautious. If I give myself to Baezal, will I not be trading one cage for another? He would never force me to remain with him, but in choosing to do so, am I not just crafting another gilded prison for myself? What about the freedom I longed for? The adventures—seeing the sea after spending years reading about it. Was it smart to relinquish all those dreams to another so soon?

Looking into Baezal's eyes, I feel those lingering doubts slip away. What is freedom if not the chance to share it with someone you care about? If I have the means to travel, would I not want to do it with Baezal by my side? My choice was made the moment he touched me. I will spend my future with him—not caged by love but freed by it.

He will not keep me as the One True Faith had or as Father Knoll tried to do. Baezal will take me on adventures, and we will make new memories together. Once I give myself to him fully, those lingering doubts will be silenced.

We are two souls once trapped by the True Faith. His prison was more literal than mine, but we have both suffered under the church. We are reclaiming our lives together. This is the first night of my freedom, and I'm spending it with the male I love.

I could've left this place the moment he agreed to help me, but I didn't. I want to be right here tonight, sharing this pitiful cot with my gargoyle, who hopefully is about to bring me even more pleasure than he had before. I want him so much I can scarcely breathe.

It's time for me to show Baezal just how much he means to me.

My fingers trail over each hard muscle of his stomach. I shiver at his power as my hands travel lower. Baezal snarls as my hands linger at the waistband of his simple cotton pants. They do nothing to conceal the monstrous length lurking inside. It rises proudly to attention. I savor his hiss as I stroke him through the material.

"Careful, I'm already on edge from resisting you while you slept."

His words send a shiver through me as I stare up into his eyes. Blinking innocently, I pump him over his pants once more. Baezal's stomach muscles tighten as he curls towards me. His wings flap swiftly.

"You have no idea the picture you made beside me. Naked, trusting, beautiful—like a sleeping angel." The veins in his neck pop as I squeeze him tightly, my heart hammering inside my ribs. "I wondered how you'd look if I slipped the sheet off your body and woke you with my cock."

I squeeze him tightly before roughly jerking him with my fist. Sweat erupts on his brow. My lips part as I turn slippery between my thighs. No male has ever brought this out in me. The way Baezal speaks to me in these heated moments inflames my lust and encourages me to meet his wanton confessions with my own.

"You could've done it—I welcome you inside me whenever you'd like," I purr.

A spray of moisture coats the front of his pants. Baezal curses, his hips thrusting in my hand. His palm comes down on my breasts, worrying my nipple into a stiff peak.

"You better mean that, Willow," he snarls. "Once I feel your virginity give way, it'll be a battle to keep from fucking you all day and night."

A giggle erupts from my throat as I pump him again.

"You can't fuck me all day long," I state matter-of-factly. "At least not every day. I'll need to eat, and sleep, and bathe, and explore this new world of ours together."

My hand slides under his waistband. Hot, hard flesh greets my hand as I pull his cock from its cotton prison. My mouth goes dry at the size of him. I have no idea how he's going to fit inside me, but I'm more than willing to try.

His light gray shaft is covered in the same delicate scales as the rest of his body. My arousal slips from me at the thought of what that will feel like. The head of his cock is a darker gray and already leaking a pearl of sticky come. I lick my lips and wrap my hand around his base. My fingers stretch, but can't seem to fit all the way around.

"Other than that, Baezal. You can fuck me as many times as you want."

With a snarl, Baezal moves as quickly as a whip. The sheet covering us is tossed away as he scrambles down the edge of the bed. Quickly shedding his pants, he is clad only in the leather cuffs around his wrists. His cock stands at attention, nearly grazing his stomach. Fresh seed spills from the tip and drips onto the bed below.

My tongue darts out as my eyes focus on his cock. Baezal shakes his head once, every muscle in his body pulled tight.

"There's no time for that."

Without another word, he hooks me under my hips and drags me to the foot of the bed. The sheets are cool against my hot skin. Tossing my knees over his shoulder, he slides between my legs.

"Next time you'll have to let me suck you," I pout.

"Next time," he agrees with a terse nod. "I have to be inside you. *Now*."

Gripping his massive length in his hand, he slaps it against my clit, causing my whole body to jerk. My pink flesh is painted with his milky seed.

He smacks me with it over and over until I'm trembling. Dragging his hardness through my folds, our mingling releases coat the head of his cock. I'm so wet he should have no problem sliding into me. My body is relaxed enough from my earlier climaxes. I'm not ignorant—my books taught me to expect a bit of pain for my first time—but I'm more eager than afraid.

The head of his cock pushes into my entrance, and my eyes nearly fall shut. Baezal grips my ankle, opening me up wider to his thrust. His invasion of me is slow and measured. I watch him strain while holding himself back. The scales of his cock glide along my inner walls and make me see stars. His cock reaches the barrier of my virginity.

Baezal curses, leaning down to capture my lips in a bruising kiss.

"Forgive me, my angel."

Laying another searing kiss on me, his hips punch forward, and he is sheathed fully inside me. The pinch of pain I felt burns as he remains still. He stretches me to the point I feel obscenely full. I kiss him back slowly, my body trying to adjust to this new sensation. There is pain—he is large, and I'm a virgin—but it quickly begins to recede.

His fingers rub my clit gently as his lips continue to work mine. My hands fall to his back, resting at the base of his wings. I hold onto them tightly, knowing things will not stay this gentle for long.

"Beautiful," Baezal sighs, before kissing my left breast. "Brave."

Words of adoration are whispered against my heated flesh. The longer he remains still, the deeper my desire becomes. The pain is gone. All I want now is for him to make good on his promise. I want to feel him every time I walk in the morning.

"Move," I encourage.

Baezal looks unsure, so I kiss him again. Pressing our foreheads together, I stare into his sapphire gaze.

"Please, Baezal. Fuck me."

Baezal growls as he kisses me one final time. Gripping my ankle tightly, he opens me wide and slides back. The feel of the scales on his cock is pure bliss. He withdraws until only his head remains in me and then thrusts forward. I groan as I'm stretched again. The feel of his girth steals my breath.

His heavy balls brush against my ass as he spears into me again. My breasts jostle at the force of his claiming. There is a primal edge to each of his movements that sets my blood on fire. My wantonness has reached new depths after tonight. To know this pleasure exists but to be bereft of it would kill me. My future is entwined with Baezal's. No one could give me the type of bliss he does.

With each thrust, the shackles of my past crumble into dust. I am reborn in this bed as the true me. Baezal pushes deep inside me, and I can taste freedom on my tongue. All I smell is him—smoke and night air. Baezal is everywhere, inside me and in my heart. In this moment, we are one. As I watch his gray cock disappear into my pink opening, I've never felt so connected to another.

I clench down on him and am rewarded by his growl.

"You have the face of an angel, but your pussy is positively unholy," he snarls, thrusting into me without reprieve. "It is the rapture and damnation all in one. A male will commit blasphemy just to worship it until the end of his days."

"Baezal," I sigh. "You feel so good. Fuck me harder. Please."

I fall back onto my elbows so I can see the whole scene more clearly. Baezal's hands go to my hips as he fucks me on and off of his length. His wings spread out behind him. We make quite a picture. A demon rutting into the deflowered

Sister—it is blasphemy, but nothing has ever felt more right in my life.

I grip the sheets around me as he powers into me. Our bodies smack together in a symphony of slapping, wet flesh. Each drag of his scales brings me closer to my peak.

"Baezal. Yes!" I scream. "You were always meant to be my first."

Madness dances in his bright eyes. His claws grip me harder until I'm sure they've pierced through my skin.

"And only."

It's the closest he's come to a confession. It sends white-hot pleasure licking up my skin. He fucks me harder than seems possible. Each thrust is deeper than the last. We slide up the bed with the force of his movements.

I nod frantically as my peak looms closer.

"I belong to you, Baezal. I'm yours."

He snarls at my words, tossing my legs over his shoulders and locking his arms around them. He powers into me from below, the fit of us even tighter than before. The monster he tries so hard to hide is out on full display. His movements are primal and claiming. I love every way he dominates me.

"Going to keep you forever, my angel. They kept you from me. Locked away in a monastery beyond my reach—they will pay for keeping us apart."

My hands fall to his powerful thighs as he lifts my bottom half completely off the bed. His fangs snap at my ankles as my vision begins to darken at the edges.

"Father Knoll wanted me for himself. Kept me there in the hopes of having me one day, but you set me free. You saved me."

My confession is broken up by sobs of pleasure. Baezal snarls, his eyes nearly entirely black.

"If that bastard ever comes looking for you, I'll kill him," he vows. "Gut him and make him watch me fuck you as his life slips away, knowing you were only ever mine."

A scream is ripped from my lungs as I clench down tightly on his thrusting cock. My climax surprises me. It was Baezal's words that had sent me over the edge. His devotion to me and the violence he vowed to inflict on the man who scared me for so long. The finality in his claim had sent me tumbling over the edge and headfirst into pleasure.

Arousal soaks us both as Baezal continues to power into me. Only once I've started to come down does he slow his thrusts. Pushing deep, he drops my legs and leans over me. Finding my mouth, he slicks his tongue against mine. My body feels like jelly. I can barely keep my eyes open, but Baezal just chuckles.

"I'm not done with you yet."

Before I can say another word, he pulls me from bed and sets me on my feet. Kissing me swiftly, he turns me towards the wall. His hands find my hips and gently tip me forward. With his help, he guides my right foot atop the barren nightstand. My palms flatten against the wall for balance.

His claws collect my sweat-soaked hair and drape it over my shoulder. I was tired before, but now, as I feel his tongue lick along my spine, I've come awake again. His knees hit the floor with a soft thud. Claws prick the cheeks of my ass as he gently spreads them apart. His tongue presses against my back entrance. I moan, my head falling against the cool stone wall.

Gently pushing his slick muscles into my asshole, I feel my breath catch. He doesn't push too far until he retreats. His tongue licks into my pussy as if in a simple greeting. Nipping both of my cheeks, I hear him rise to his feet. His cock lines up with my entrance, and he enters me in one hard thrust.

It's tighter this way. I have no doubt I'll be sore tomorrow, and I welcome the discomfort. Arching my back, he pulls my hips away from the wall and kicks my feet apart. He powers into me, my ass cushioning the cradle of his hips. His scales drag inside me, the rhythm bordering between pleasure and pain.

His lips find my ear.

"Do you like this, sweet Willow?" he whispers. "Being fucked by a monster like you are his plaything."

I nod, my forehead scraping against the wall.

"I love it."

Baezal chuckles darkly, his hand raises to wrap around the length of my hair. He snatches my head back. My scalp prickles on the very edge of discomfort.

"My angel doesn't act like a virgin. She opens her legs wider for me—begs me to take her harder." His teeth bite into my neck, and I scream, clenching down on his cock. "You are a wanton woman—a vixen. You were forged in the flames of desire and need a rough fucking to keep you satisfied."

My mouth opens on a moan. I look up at him, knowing what needs to be said to send us both falling deep into pleasure.

"And you think you'll be able to keep me satiated?"

Baezal's grin is pure male satisfaction. His hand slips over my hip and begins working circles on my clit. My breath catches, pleasure licks at my sweaty skin. When this next climax comes, it will decimate me more than the first one.

"I'll keep you well fucked and cared for until the end of time. Pleasure will be the only thing you know." His eyes blaze into mine. "The next time I fuck you, you'll beg me to do it. Like a good girl with my cock in your mouth."

His fingers continue to work my clit. My whole body begins to tremble as he powers into me.

"B—Baezal, I'm close."

"Then come for me. Tighten your pretty cunt on my cock, and I'll reward you with my seed."

His thrusts become sloppy as my peak looms close. I work

my hips backwards, meeting his thrusts with my own. He is impossibly deep.

"Come inside me, please, my love. I want it."

The words slip from my lips, and my confession sends us both off the cliff. Shoving himself deep inside me, his fingers worry my clit until I erupt. I clench down on him hard as my body shakes with the force of my climax. Baezal thrusts into me one final time before his chest molds to my back. A torrent of hot seed fills me to the point of overflowing.

His sticky come trails down my inner thighs as he fuck the last of it into me. His lips trail open-mouth kisses along my shoulder. At last, I feel him fully withdraw. Immediately, I want him back. I can feel the phantom impression of him inside me. My heart reaches for his as my soul longs for the two of us to be entwined.

Gently, he turns me from the wall and settles me atop the mussed sheets. He disappears for a moment to retrieve a cloth and clean his release from my skin. Tossing the used rag aside, I open my arms for him to fall against me. Baezal chuckles as he rolls us into the center of the bed. I hum deep in my throat, too content to worry about him not returning my sentiments. I called him my love because he is, whether he feels the same or not.

I won't let his silence ruin this perfect night. If he's not ready yet, then I will gladly wait until he is.

The room grows dim as the candles burn nearly to their stumps. Our sweaty skin sticks together. Tiredness makes my body feel like mush. My eyelids grow heavy as I nuzzle deeper into his chest.

"That was perfect," I murmur against his throat.

I feel Baezal smile as his hands skim along my back.

"Not nearly as perfect as you."

His hands pause, and I feel him swallow against my cheek. His lips caress my temple.

"*My love.*"

I smile wider into his chest, humming with happiness. Two simple words have changed everything. There is no need to worry about my future. With Baezal's arms around me, I am safe, cared for, and loved.

For the first time in decades, I don't worry about locking the door to my room. Baezal will protect me from everything. The only cage I'll find myself in is the one made of Baezal's strong arms.

My love's heart pounds in time with my own. It is the most perfect lullaby that leads me into the waiting darkness.

6

WILLOW

Sunlight streams into my eyes from a few uneven slats in the ceiling.

Golden rays pour over the simple room. The scent of damp has returned. With a yawn, I stretch my arms over my head, already feeling the stiffness of my muscles. The ache makes me think of Baezal.

Rolling over, I find his side of the bed empty. The sheets are still warm, meaning he must've recently left them. Hopefully, he journeyed to find us some breakfast. I'm ravenous this morning after all the lovemaking we did last night. The tenderness between my thighs brings a smile to my face.

I've never felt more at peace than I do now. Everything feels perfect.

We should set out after we eat today. Leave this abandoned church behind and find somewhere with a real bed. Once we are free of here, we can start our own adventure. There are no more doubts between us. He called me his love.

Baezal is every bit the valiant knight come to rescue me. His armor is merely the scales on his skin.

Our fates have been written and woven together in a

tapestry of love. Never again will we suffer under the One True Faith. Baezal has been freed from his stony prison, and I will never see Father Knoll or Sister Grayvle again.

Even as I feel certain of the fact, apprehension begins to trickle into my stomach. Especially as the minutes pass and Baezal still has not returned. Growing restless, I fling back the sheet and stretch out fully. The stone floor is cold against my naked feet.

My stomach growls, and while I'm hungry for food, a more potent hunger for my gargoyle is beginning to over take it.

I catch my appearance in the small mirror atop the vanity. I look like me, but I've also changed. There are red bite marks along my throat and shoulders. My lips are swollen. Indentations from his claws decorate my ass, while his lingering seed has dried onto my thighs.

I look as if I've been thoroughly ravaged by a beast, and I guess that's not too far off from the truth. A flush rises to my cheeks. I should bathe, but not yet. Perhaps Baezal and I can—

A door slams from above me as footsteps creak along the floorboards. My early worry melts away at the return of my love.

"Baezal!" I call, hoping that if he knows I'm awake, he'll return to me fast.

Indeed, his footsteps seem to pick up the pace as I hear them descend down the stairs. My anticipation grows, feeling as if I haven't seen him in years rather than just hours. I'd happily forgo breakfast just to have him devour me instead.

"My love, I've woken up in desperate need to be taken thoroughly by my gargoyle again."

Movement in the doorway catches my attention. My grin widens as I turn from the vanity.

"Did you manage to—"

The question dies on my tongue as I take in the figure looming just outside my room. Ice collects in my veins as bile races up my throat. At first, I'm tempted to believe I'm stuck in a nightmare. One that my love will soon rouse me from with his soft kisses.

However, I know in my heart that this is all too real. Baezal has not returned to me.

Prowling into my room is none other than Father Knoll.

His beady eyes narrow in on me. Thinning, dark hair plasters to his head. The white robes he wears are lightly stained around the edges. His ruddy, pot-marked skin sags with age. Father Knoll's thin lips pull back in a sneer, baring his yellow teeth at me.

I scream, watching in disgust as his eyes travel down my naked body. Gripping the sheet on the bed, I wrap it around myself. The anger in his eyes turns to rage.

All the color drains from my face as I stumble back against the wall. Father Knoll prowls into the room, leather-bound prayer book in hand. He thrusts it towards me, veins bulging at his neck.

"I came to offer you salvation, child. Offer you the chance to pay penance for your lustful ways." He wrinkles his nose in disgust. "I thought a night spent alone in hunger would make you more agreeable to the life I could give you. The life of a Sister."

Coming fully into the room, he is only a few feet from me. I can smell his putrid body odor. Saliva collects at the corners of his mouth.

"Instead, I find a whore where a Sister was left. A deviant—who allowed herself to be defiled by a creature."

His eyes fall to the bed. The crimson stain of my virginity lingers on the mattress. I swallow thickly, my stomach threatening to upend its contents.

"No human man would've left those marks on you. Have you strayed so far in your sinful ways that you cavorted with a beast?"

I open my mouth, but fear steals my voice. Father Knoll shakes his head and tosses his prayer book atop the bed. Stomping towards me, his hands go to the buckle of his pants.

"It would seem the only way to save you is to treat you as all vile women should be. A show of force might do you some good."

My head feels dizzy, but I cannot afford to pass out. Not now. I have no weapon, no exit, but I still have the means to fight him.

Why had we not left last night? Where has Baezal gone? Has he abandoned me after all? Gotten what he wanted and fled in the morning light, never to be seen again. Were all his vows hollow?

It isn't possible. He is my protector—my knight—he would never—

"I can see you beginning to understand," Father Knoll sighs, his belt hitting the stone floor with a metallic clank. "The beast fucked you, gave you his putrid seed, and left? Of course he did. What use would a demon have for a lecherous whore beyond the pleasures of the flesh?"

Father Knoll is within arm's reach. I look around, desperate for anything to arm myself with, but this room is heartbreakingly bare. His polished boots nearly brush my toes. His scent makes my stomach roll. Yellow, cracked teeth grin down at me.

"Only I can save you. Only I love you. Repay my kindness over the years, Sister Willow, by keeping quiet and letting me enjoy this."

Reaching down, I close my eyes and twist away. Fear freezes me, and any thoughts to flee are wiped from my mind. I brace myself for his disgusting touch, hoping there will be some kind of opening for me to break free of his grasp. As the moments pass and I don't feel his clammy skin, I crack one eye open.

The spot where Father Knoll had once stood is empty. I blink, trying to comprehend what has just happened. There is a wet thud out in the hallway, followed by a muffled scream. Rising on shaking knees, I tuck the sheet around myself and pad out into the hallway.

The sight that greets me is gruesome. Still, my heart lifts at the sight of familiar gray skin. Baezal has returned, his wings proud and splaying from his back. The sunlight streaming in from the stairwell illuminates the sharp angles of his face. A forgotten sack of food rests against the wall, along with the bloody scene at his feet.

Father Knoll trembles against the stone floor. Blood spills from his mouth as he presses a hand to his stomach. The fleshy contents of his organs seep between his splayed fingers. His white robes are just as scarlet as the ones I arrived in. Blood soaks the floor beneath him as he weakly murmurs for mercy.

Baezal's claws curl around Father Knoll's thick jaw.

"You came back here to scare her—to hurt her. Returning was a mistake, and you will pay for it with your life." He snarls down into the other man's face. "You will die here. For keeping her caged, my hands will bring about your end."

"Baezal," I breathe, stepping fully into the hall.

His head whips towards me, dark hair spilling over his shoulder. My breath catches on a sob as moisture pricks at my eyes. He wipes his bloody hands on the wall before approaching me. I can't contain myself and launch into his arms. He catches me up against him, smoothing down the sheet around me as if in need of a physical reminder that I'm okay.

"Willow." He says my name like a prayer. "I'm so sorry, my love. I only left to find breakfast for you. I never should have abandoned you here, defenseless. Your fear— I felt it and nearly went out of my mind thinking that I didn't get to you in time and—"

"Shhh," I whisper, pressing my hands to his chest. "You saved me, Baezal. *Again.*"

"Always."

The softness in his gaze turns hard as he looks over to Father Knoll. His ruddy complexion has gone shockingly pale. His breathing is ragged. The stench of death is already upon him.

"Let me end this."

Biting my lip, I mull over his words. Ever since I was a girl, I've been afraid of Father Knoll. Afraid of him noticing the changes in my body or being caught alone with him in his study. He preyed upon me just like he had dozens of other Sisters in the monastery. He was the real monster, not Baezal.

Father Knoll always seemed to be this imposing figure—wielding enough power to make him dangerous. Now, as his death looms, he is just a man. A pathetic one at that. The fear of him I once had melts away, replaced by resolve. He is my greatest demon to overcome, the one I need to conquer to be free of my past.

There's only one thing to do—reclaim what he had attempted to take from me. He would die knowing no part of me ever belonged to him. I have a lover who will kill for me.

Father Knoll will be his first victim.

A smile curls my lips as I cup Baezal's cheek and drag his eyes back to me. Meeting his mouth with mine, I moan into our kiss. Licking his lips, I slip my tongue into his mouth, savoring his groan. His hands fall to my back, holding me close. His straining erection presses into my stomach. Rubbing against it, arousal coats the inside of my thighs.

Father Knoll makes a sound of protest from the floor. His wheezing becomes more pronounced. Breaking our kiss, I lick my lips and stare up at my savior.

"Remember what you said last night? You'd gut him if he returned for me." I nod towards the dying man on the floor. "Which you've already accomplished."

My hand slips down his chest before palming him through his pants.

"Don't you want to make him watch you fuck me?"

"Willow," Baezal groans, but I'm already sliding to my knees.

The sheet cushions my naked skin from the hard floor. Staring up at him, I press up on my knees, kissing the hard outline of his cock through his pants. Wetness greets my mouth, and Baezal groans.

"Please let me suck your cock first, my love. I want to earn my fucking."

The sheet slips off my shoulder as I slide the waistband of his pants down his hips. His erection springs free, and my eyes widen at the tremendous sight.

"My angel," Baezal groans, but makes no move to stop me.

Fisting his cock, I roughly pump him as best I can. Licking my lips, I grin up at him.

"Cease t—this vile act at once," Father Koll spits. Blood pours down his chin. "Get me some help. I demand it."

We both ignore him as my tongue snakes out and leaks at the drop of seed at his tip. I groan at his salty sweetness. My tongue licks over the dark head, tasting him fully. Above me, Baezal curses.

"Good girl, Willow. Deeper now. As far as you can."

Growing bolder with his praise, I open my mouth wide enough for my cheeks to ache. Flattening my tongue, I take his length deep into my mouth. I run my tongue only his scales as his hands grip my scalp. His cock hits the back of my throat, causing tears to flood my eyes. I hold him there for as long as I can until I choke, saliva coating his length. I use it to help my other hand pump him as I slide him out of my mouth.

"You taste so good." I pump him roughly against my tongue. "It's making me wet."

Licking along his scales, Baezal's stomach muscles jump. He

pants as his claws prick my scalp. It's not long before his hips begin to move, meeting my mouth with thrusts. I lick the underside of his cock and the seam of his balls. I press kisses along the shaft and take him down my throat once more.

"Fuck, Willow. You're so good at this. Have you done it before?"

He knows my answer, but this is all part of his claiming. Pulling him from my throat, I use the tip of his cock to smear seed and spit along my lips. Leaning back on my heels, I shake my head primly.

"Only for you."

His wings flare behind him in pleasure. Wrapping my hair in his fist, he turns towards Father Knoll, who still draws rasping breath. I return his cock, licking and biting down on his impressive length.

"Only me, that's right." His hips slide forward, pushing him deeper into my mouth. "Look at how she sucks my cock, Father. A beast you called me—well, she certainly makes me one. It's a beast that satisfies her perfect little pussy. It's a beast that knows what she looks like when she comes. Not you."

His words kindle a fire within me. My pussy clenches around nothing, desperate to be filled again. I suck him faster, pumping him even more roughly with my hand. My motions are frantic. I try to cram as much of him in my mouth as I can. His hands lock around my head and hold me still. He punches his hips forward, then retreats. I relax my jaw and let him take his pleasure.

He fucks my face just as ruthlessly as he does my pussy.

"You'll die without ever knowing such pleasure. You'll die knowing the one you desire most belongs to me—a monster."

Baezal thrusts deep, and I gag on him. Pulling out, more saliva and seed decorate my mouth and drip down my chin. Staring into my eyes, I see adoration shining in his blue gaze.

It's the same love I have for him reflecting down at me. I turn towards Father Knoll, glancing at him for the last time.

"You'll die knowing that I love a gargoyle with my entire being. My heart and soul are his."

A spray of come decorates my chest as Baezal groans. Staring up at him, he quickly snatches me into his arms. His mouth descends on mine. Our tongues dance together in a now familiar rhythm. Once we are both breathless, we pull apart.

"I love you, too. You broke my curse—you are my fate. And my fate is to love and protect you for all eternity."

His vow is sealed with a kiss. It's perfect—my very own, albeit a bit unorthodox, happily ever after. What more could a girl wish for?

Kissing me one last time, he reluctantly lets me go. I watch him stomp over Father Knoll, but my eyes never travel to that wretched man again. Baezal leans down, voice deadly soft.

"One final question before this is all over, Father."

"Rot in hell," Father Knoll spits.

"Things can always get worse for you, Father. Remember that. Let's try this again. Where can I find the True Blessed Father?"

There is a brief pause. For a moment, I don't think Father Knoll is going to answer him, until I hear a harsh choking sound.

"He's dead."

Baezal tsks.

"Try again."

A soft squelching sound echoes in the hallways. Father Knoll screams as Baezal digs into his open stomach. The metallic scent of blood eclipses all others in the hallway.

"Fine. Fine!" Father Knoll shouts. "I'll tell you."

His response is too low for me to hear. Satisfied, my gargoyle nods. My eyes meet Baezal's burning gaze.

"You don't get to watch me fuck her."

With that final edict, Baezal clasps the other man's hand between his two strong hands. There is a sharp snap, followed by a sickening thud. The figure on the floor never moves again.

Father Knoll is dead. My relief is palpable.

Rising from the floor, Baezal gently walks over to me. His arms wrap around me and I rest my cheek against his chest.

"You're safe, Willow."

"How many times are you going to have to save me?" I ask with a smile.

"As many as it takes."

Baezal chuckles as he lifts a hand. He cringes at the sight of Father Knoll's blood staining his fingers.

"We should bathe," I offer.

With a nod, Baezal leads me deeper down the hallway. A modest bathroom is located near the back, fitted with a simple porcelain tub. With a wave of his hand, steaming water fills the basin. Baezal helps me shed my sheet and carefully lowers me into the water.

The water is delicious and soothes my stiff muscles. I settle against him at the far end of the tub. His wings hang off the side as his fingers gently strum up and down my arm. With another wave of his hand, a bar of pine-scented soap appears in his palm. He drags it along my skin, and I shiver.

"Where do you want to go from here, Willow? I'll take you anywhere."

I hum deep in my throat, sighing as his hands slip between my thighs.

"Somewhere with a beach. I've always wanted to visit the sea."

Baezal smiles down at me.

"I know just the place."

Setting the soap aside, I turn in his lap. My hands grip his shoulders as my thighs go to the other side of his hips. His erection teases my entrance, but I have to stay focused. I cannot give in to my desires just yet.

"I need to do something first."

"What is it?"

I smile against his mouth.

"You'll see."

Once we are both clean enough, Baezal plucks me from the water and carries my dripping body back towards our room. Without delay, he sheathes himself inside me. Our souls fuse together as one. Our connection is permanent. We make love until the sun begins to set, and our rumbling stomachs cannot be ignored.

Tomorrow we will embark on our new adventure, but there is one final demon from my past that needs to be eradicated before I can move on with my new life.

Well, maybe two.

7

WILLOW

Watching dozens of my Sisters flee Thorncatcher Monastery without so much as a backward glance warms my heart.

To be fair, there wouldn't be any reason for them to stay. The once-proud structure, with its wrought-iron steeples, now sits smoldering. With each passing minute, large swaths of the building crumble in on itself, blanketing the grass with ash.

It was hard coming back here. If I'm being honest, I nearly didn't do it. If Father Knoll had not come to Shadowveil Church yesterday, I'm certain I would've left with Baezal and never thought of this place again. However, my confrontation with him had left me rattled. I knew I couldn't embark on my new life before settling the score of my last one.

I was far from the only Sister Father Knoll targeted. His lecherous deeds were whispered about long before I arrived here. Countless Sisters have suffered within these walls. Now that they, too, have been freed, they can do as they please. Whether that is to rejoin another order or start a life far from the True Faith, the choice is theirs.

The only one not getting to decide her future is Sister Grayvle. She is just as guilty as Father Knoll. She was his dutiful aide who led to the suffering of so many women and girls. With Baezal's help, I made sure her cruelty would never harm another.

Currently, she sits bound and gagged in the monastery's cellar. She'll be lucky if the rats eat her before the flames claim her.

As each figure draped in white hurries through the open gate, peace settles inside me. Watching them go, I know I made the right decision to return. I've given them all the same gift I was: a choice. Without my action, Sister Grayvle would've found a replacement for Father Knoll. One who was just as cruel.

Baezal stands beside me, watching the Sisters leave silently. Rescuing them would've been impossible without his help. Some had been wary upon his arrival—they were all taught the same lies about gargoyles as I was. That apprehension faded once they saw the depth of his kindness.

At some point during the day, I fell even more in love with him. A feat I didn't know was possible.

Turning towards me, a soft evening breeze blows the silky strands of his hair. Dusk has fallen, and the stars twinkle above us, dancing in their indigo sky.

"Ready to go?" he asks, twining his arm around my waist.

The leather strap of my satchel digs into his large chest. I took a few things with me before we torched the monastery. My personal effects had luckily remained untouched during my time in confinement. There were only a few pieces I wished to take with me into my new life.

My most valued being my well-loved, dog-eared copy of *The Knight's Heart*, packed carefully inside. Additionally, I managed to save a few drawings and coins we pilfered from Father Knoll's office. Each Sister had been given a decent sum from his deep coffers. It was enough for them to procure safe passage wherever they wished to go.

I smile up at Baezal, pressing my palms to his strong chest.

"There's one last thing I want to show you before I never return to this place again."

Smoke hangs heavy in the air as I take Baezal's hand in mine and lead him away from the burning building. The soft grass snags at the hem of my green gown. It doesn't take long for us to reach the small garden nestled under a willow tree. It's where I was left as a baby. The Sisters who discovered me saw it fitting to name me after the tree that guarded me through the night.

That's why I've always felt attached to the patch of land here. All manner of wildflowers bloom from the beds. Golds, pinks, purples, and blues create a cacophony of colors. They grow tall with sturdy stems, broken up only by the straight sprigs of lavender. The scent is heavenly.

"This was the only happy place I had here," I sigh. "I tended to it every day for hours. It's the only place I'll miss. I put so much love into it."

Baezal's hand cups my cheek, drawing my eyes up towards him. His expression is soft, a look of understanding kindling in his gaze. I smile up at him, ignoring the stinging in my eyes.

"I want to give it a proper goodbye."

Pressing up on my toes, I meet his mouth with mine. Our kiss is soft, reverent, and sets my blood on fire.

"Make love to me," I command.

Baezal chuckles, his hand slipping under the satchel strap and gently tossing it aside. His hands return to my waist, lifting me slightly. The toes of my slippers barely brush the grass as he kisses me again. Our tongues twin together in a familiar dance.

"Of course, my angel."

I laugh into his mouth.

"I knew you wouldn't be opposed to the idea."

Baezal wastes no time. His claws easily sever the laces of my gown until the heavy material pools at my feet. The cool breeze teases my naked skin as I kick the discarded dress away. His hands slide down my back, kneading every mound of flesh he can find. I moan into his mouth, kissing him hard. My teeth sink into his lower lip and bite gently.

My gargoyle's eyes flash as his claws press into my skin. With a snarl, he lays me down atop my bed of flowers and lavender. The blooms cushion my back as I lie awaiting my lover's touch. His wings spread behind him, nearly blotting out the full moon. Stars dance above him.

Holding my breath, I watch him shed his pants. The sight of his massive cock always takes me aback. Moisture surges from between my thighs in anticipation of his claiming. Baezal lowers down atop me, his scales sliding against my hard nipples. I moan, rubbing myself against him as our mouths reconnect.

Hooking my arms and legs around him, I roll Baezal onto his back. Many flowers are crushed in the process, but their fragrance only heightens my arousal. Being on top is new for me. The angle at which we kiss is different as well. My tongue dips into his mouth as his hands grip my hips. Rubbing me against his straining erection, wetness coats his length.

My clit is desperate for more friction as I work myself against him.

"Your greedy pussy needs to be reminded of who owns it."

"It's yours," I sigh.

His claws prick into my ass, dragging me up his strong body. I aid him by sitting up. His hands go to my waist, and mine fall to his chest to keep myself steady. His pupils widen as he looks up at me. The lower half of his face is hidden by my body.

"Watch what I do to you, my angel. Watch as I feast on your cunt."

The first lick of his tongue sends my screams careening

through the willow tree. The firm glide of his wet muscle sets my body on fire. Throwing my head back, my fingers sinking into his chest. Soft scales tickle my palm.

Baezal makes good on his word and devours me. My hips canter onto his tongue. Spearing it inside me, I writhe, making it push deeper. He fucks me with it slowly, bringing me closer to the edge with each soft thrust. Claws grip my ass, gently pulling it apart. Wickedness gleams in his eyes as he shifts me forward.

Licking slower, the tip of his tongue jiggles at my back entrance. I scream as it gently spears into me. Satisfied with his invasion, Baezal gives my ass a soft slap before working me against his tongue. My thighs begin to tremble on each side of his face.

"Baezal—I'm—I—"

"Come for me, sweet Willow. Let your Sisters hear you."

His lips close around my clit and suck deep. Tossing my head back, I climax right on top of him. Moisture flows from me and soaks his face and chest. My eyes are wide, but I barely see the sky above me. Pure bliss flows through my veins. Screams of pleasure echo around us.

Baezal licks me thoroughly, not missing one drop of my spend. Still shaking, I slide down his body. My sweaty skin clings to his as we share a soft kiss. I taste myself on his tongue. Sweet and salty, a heady combination. Our tongues gently glide together as we savor the tender moment.

His cock rests heavy against my stomach. I can feel sticky seed glistening from the tip. I rub against him, fire growing in his blue eyes. Mustering the rest of my strength, I loom over him. Taking his length in my hand, I drag my fist up and down his hard shaft.

"What are you going to do with my cock?" Baezal asks through clenched teeth.

I grin up at him, letting my hair curl around my breasts.

Rising up on my knees, I drag his cock through my wet folds until the head glistens. Gripping him tightly, I position him at my entrance.

"Put it back where it belongs."

I punctuate my words by sinking fully down on his hardness. The stretch is instant, and my teeth grind together. Baezal's growl of pleasure echoes around us in the garden. Being on top provides an interesting view. Placing my hands on his chest, I watch his face contort with pleasure. His claws dig into my hips as he raises them, encouraging me to fuck myself fast on his length.

"Such a perfect pussy. Look at how well you take my cock."

I slam down onto his lap with a moan.

"Only yours."

His eyes blaze as I rise up. Bringing myself down, he lifts his hips to greet me, spearing even deeper inside. His cock butts up against my womb. The scales of his shaft tickle a secret spot inside me that has my pleasure looming closer.

"That's right. Mine. Mine to love. Mine to keep." He slams into, causing my breasts to bounce. "Mine to fuck."

"Baezal, Baezal, *Baezal*," I babble uncontrollably.

His fingers sneak between us and find my clit. With a few tight circles, I sink down on him with a scream. My pussy clenches around his hardness. White fire licks at my sink as pleasure erupts. Baezal snarls, his hips come clean off the ground. My pleasure numbs me. I'm barely aware we've moved until Baezal has me in his arms and we're launching into the sky.

I don't have enough strength to scream. Not has his massive wings hold us aloft. The moon and stars look close enough to touch. Holding me under my ass, my knees fall into the crook of his elbows.

"Feel me. Come again and let the whole world hear your pleasure."

The command is growled against my throat. He fucks me ruthlessly as I hold on for dear life. When his teeth sink into my flesh, I erupt again. The bit of pain tosses me overboard into a sea of pleasure. I clench down on him, biting his neck for good measure.

Baezal snarls against my throat and thrusts deep, emptying himself inside me. Each hot torrent of his seed sends small shocks of pleasure through me. The wind whips against us as we stay afloat.

"You are so beautiful, Willow," Baezal whispers against my ear.

My face warms, and I burrow into his neck. After all we shared, it's shocking I can still feel shy. Baezal chuckles, holding me close.

"All the creatures who call *The Woods* home must be looking up at us with envy. Wondering to themselves as to how I've gotten lucky enough to claim you. And you are claimed. My seed drips from your little cunt. My teeth mar your lovely neck. You are mine. Forever."

Our souls thread together as our hearts beat as one. All my life, I was looking for my freedom—the chance to really be myself. Every sin, every mistake, every risk led me right here, to Baezal. It was all worth it. I've found my knight—my love. I'll never feel alone again. I can be exactly who I am and he'll love me for it.

Fiercely.

"Forever," I agree, pressing our foreheads together. "Now take me to the sea."

Baezal's chuckle echoes through the night sky. We descend only briefly to collect our clothing and my satchel of trinkets. We fly far away from Thorncatcher Monastery, and I never look back.

Not even once.

The heavy padlock glistens in the setting sun.

Thick, iron chains drag the leather bag deep below the dark waves. It doesn't take long for it to disappear from view. The contents and the shackles are heavy enough to drag it into the sea. Salty air coats my tongue, tempered only by the scent of lavender.

Willow is beside me. The brackish wind blows her dark hair behind her. The soft strands tangle in my scales. Her breasts rest atop my forearms as I hold her from behind. I always need her but especially in this moment. We haven't spent a day apart since the curse broke. Each day we find a new way to love each other. The depth of our desire never wanes.

The shackles of the past have been broken. Anyone who sought to cage us has now been dealt with.

As we stand and watch the body of the True Blessed Father sink below the water, I feel a sense of peace wash over me. I would've been happy never getting my revenge. Life with Willow is sweet enough to forget all the horrors I endured. However, in the end, I could not let him draw breath. It weighed on me, especially with the knowledge that no other gargoyles had been freed from their stone prisons.

He had to pay, but I had to be smart about it.

It took some time to devise a plan. The journey to his remote monastery nearly took half a year. Though that could be because Willow and I stopped to make a home in every village we travelled through. I swear there isn't a town anywhere along the coastline where I haven't made her come. In the snow, on beaches, deep in *The Woods* with the stars and animals as our witnesses, I have claimed her thoroughly in each differing terrain.

Once we arrived at the monastery, we had to be smart. The True Blessed Father wielded dark magic. Had I known the full extent of his power, I wouldn't have been so quick to barter away some of Willow's favorite jewels to that bastard demon of *The Woods*. Even as I think it, I realize there isn't a sum I wouldn't give or a deal I wouldn't make for Willow's immortality.

As the years turned, and I watched the subtle changes in her, I knew I couldn't lose her—not to something as simple as time. Seeking out the demon had been easy enough. He wasn't nearly as frightening as the stories of him portrayed.

Especially not when his human mate encouraged him to be nice during our meeting. She and Willow had chatted animatedly, and I caught the demon's wistful stare at his mate more times than I'm sure he wanted me to. His mate had been pregnant with their child, and it made me wonder what Willow would look like carrying ours.

I was not ready to share her with anyone just yet. One day, though, it would be nice to hold a product of our love. No matter what that child would look like, it would surely be just as perfect as its mother.

When the body does not rise in some act of God from the water, Willow leans fully back against my chest, breathing deep. He's gone—that final ghost of the past laid to rest. Staring out at the dark waves, a flash of white catches my eye. Willow gasps, immediately snapping forward to attention.

The small sailboat rocks us gently on the waves. Our dutiful captain is away, paid handsomely to not ask questions about what we brought on board and why we needed to dump it this far from shore. After this, we were heading south, to the land of white sand beaches and limestone castles with towers reaching into the clouds.

After we have our fill of the beach, we could travel to the snowy mountains and keep ourselves warm by the fire all day. My cock kicks to life at the idea, pressing firmly against Willow's backside. She is too entranced by the figure in the water to notice my hardening flesh.

I wrap my cloak around us, sparing her exposed skin from the harsh wind. It was another gift from the demon that made traveling easier. To everyone beyond Willow, I would look and sound like a human man. She was the only one who saw my true form, and that's how I wanted it to be.

Gripping the railing in her fist, she turns to look at me over her shoulder.

"Is that what I think it is?"

I nod once, grabbing her by the hips and pulling our bodies closer. She shivers. Whether from my arousal or the wind, I cannot be sure.

"A merman? Yes, it has to be." I nod towards the water. "They are rare. This one is far from home."

"I wouldn't want to face his father's ire."

"Or his mother's. I fear she is even more fearsome than the Kraken of the Darksea," I add.

The white head dips below the water. When it does not resurface after several minutes, Willow sighs. Turning, she wraps her arms around me before looking up.

"How do you feel?"

"At peace." I wrap a tendril of her hair around my claw. "My revenge has been seen to. The anchors of those who wronged me no longer moor me in the dark waters of my past."

Willow wrinkles her delicate nose.

"Your affinity for poetry books is beginning to annoy."

Laughter booms from my chest as I pull her close. Pressing a kiss to her forehead, I inhale her floral scent.

"I'm glad that rotten bastard is dead. I hope the fish make a meal out of him. Better?"

"Much."

Her lips find mine in a searing press. Their pillowy softness haunts me while I sleep. I dream of every part of her, desperate to taste her over and over again. My tongue glides along her lips, and she eagerly parts them. I taste her, fully savoring the taste of wine on her tongue from dinner.

Breaking our kiss, her eyes gleam wickedly as she licks her lips.

"Come along," she states, taking my hand in hers. "It's time for bed."

I follow her dutifully, knowing sleep is the farthest thing from her mind.

In the five years we've been together, I've learned Willow inside and out. I know what scares her, what makes her cry, and of course, what brings her the most pleasure. Her wantonness has grown tenfold over the last half-decade. It is a joy and privilege to be the one who satisfies her.

I've lost count of all the times I've awoken to my cock already halfway down her throat. I do the same to her, rousing her from sleep with my mouth on her sweet pussy as the morning light paints her rosy. Once she is awake, that's when the true pleasure begins. I feast on her flesh and cunt—I swallow down her moans and come. I wring her body of every possible pleasure it could experience and then do it all over again.

I know every hidden detail of Willow from the faint scar on her hipbone to the hidden freckle behind her ear.

As I watch her elegantly guide along the ship's deck back towards our room, my blood heats in anticipation of possessing her again. It's in these moments of passionate clarity that I give thanks for the One True Faith. Not because I believe what they preached—the orchestrators of such a religion can rot for all I care—but I give thanks because it brought me to Willow.

I would give anything—even if it meant being cursed again —to spare her from the harsh realities of her past. To know how much she suffered behind those walls makes me wish I could bring Father Knoll back just to kill him again. Each time I suggest it, she says not to bother, the past is the past.

And Willow is right. Always.

The One True Faith brought us together, gave us bonds to break free. Only we could understand how the other has suffered. Willow is my fate—the other half of my soul.

Willow's body was made by angels, but her soul is pure wickedness. It is an honor to worship it every day. The setting sun frames her in gold, making her look even more heavenly than usual. I live every day for her. I've killed for her and would gladly do so again.

I love her. It's as simple as that.

A wave of possessiveness overcomes me. The moment Willow unlocks the room to our small quarters, I pounce on her. Kicking the wooden door shut behind me, I tackle her onto the bed. Her giggles echo around the room and I quickly devour them. My hands are frantic on the bodice of her dress. My sharp claws slice through fabric and boning until her breasts spill free.

Willow gasps at my aggression. Her eyes become heavy as I take one pert nipple into my mouth. Her moans are sweeter than honey. Arching off the bed, she holds my face in her hands as I suckle her. Letting her nipple go with a pop, I quickly turn my attention to the other.

"Baezal, I love when you act like this. Take me rough, my love. Claim me."

I growl, too feral to use words. Hiking her skirts up around her hips, my palm slaps down on her feminine flesh. She keens at the stinging. My angel needs a bit of pain with her pleasure. Her wetness coats my palm. I can already smell her dripping. My pants fall to my knees as I take my length in my hand.

Smearing come across the tip, I line it up with her pink opening. In one hard thrust, I'm fully seated inside her. Willow gasps, her blunt nails clutching at my shoulders. Staring down at our conjoined bodies, a flush breaks out across her cheeks. Her round breasts jostle as I fuck her ruthlessly.

Gripping her hips in my hands, I hold her steady as I unleash myself upon her little cunt. She meets each of my thrusts. I can feel her quickening on my thrusting cock. She's close, good. My claws find her clit and rub tight circles on it. Her eyes go wide, and her head falls back, nearly smacking into the wall.

Her pussy grips me like a fist as she screams my name. Arousal coats my cock as I fuck her through her climax. Once she has come down and is limp on the bed, I cease my movements. I'm careful not to spill my seed as I settle atop her. I want to give her more pleasure before I take my own tonight even if my seed is begging to fill her once again.

Beneath me, Willow continues to shiver. Quite jerkily. Pulling back with concern, I find her staring up at me with amusement in her eyes. She had been laughing. Narrowing my eyes, my thumb rubs along her swollen lips.

"What do you find so amusing, my love?"

Willow gestures between our bodies.

"Look at us. We didn't even bother to undress. It appears as if you've just plucked me from the street and thoroughly ravished me, before sending me on my way."

Chuckling, I take her mouth in mine. My hands find her ruined dress and slip it down her supple body. Her naked skin cushions my scales. Kicking my pants and cloak off, my hand falls to her breast. I test its weight in my palm, plumping it up to deliver kisses.

"Well, I'm certainly not sending you on your way. Far from it."

Willow rolls her eyes.

"I know that look."

"What?" I feign innocence. "Can't a male help his wife undress anymore?"

My wife.

The term rolls off my tongue. We had married a few months after freeing the Sisters from Thorncatcher Monastery. It had not been a religious ceremony. No one else attended, save us and the woodland creatures who found us in the clearing. Our vows had been to each other. A binding of our souls and hearts as one—a permanent declaration that we were forever. It's one of my most cherished memories.

Once we are both naked, Willow leans back on her elbows. I take the time to survey her body as if it is the first time I'm seeing it. Full breasts, soft stomach, and hips that make my mouth water. Red dances along her knees and chest. When my eyes return to her face, she wears a bemused expression.

"You want to fuck my ass."

I open my mouth to protest, but only a huff of laughter comes out. My angel knows me well.

"Is that so wrong?"

"You're too transparent."

Willow shakes her head, but is already rolling onto her stomach. The pale globes of her ass are highlighted by the candlelight. Faint impressions of my hand and teeth mar her otherwise unblemished skin. I grin as she pushes up on her knees. Leaning behind her on the bed, I spread her cheeks wide and glimpse her tight pucker.

My tongue snakes out and licks at her back entrance. Willow shivers, her fingers curling into the sheets. I dip into her little hole and savor her scream of pleasure. She's tight everywhere, but here especially. I lick my way in and out of it, loosening her just enough so she'll be able to welcome my cock. Spitting onto her pink flesh, I glide my finger through her wet pussy and use her come and my saliva to help me ease the digit inside.

Her breath catches.

"I have to give all your holes equal attention," I state. "Wouldn't want any of them feeling neglected."

"How chivalrous of you," she moans as I add a second finger. "Do you have a favorite?"

I chuckle at her question. Our shared wickedness is on full display this evening.

"No, they're each perfect."

I bite into her ass, and she groans. Her thighs are already shaking, and we've barely begun. I never last long in her ass, and frankly, neither does she. Despite her playing coy, she loves it just as much as I do.

My cock is still slick with her arousal. The bed creaks as I rise onto my knees behind her. Lining up my tip with her back entrance, I hold my breath as I slowly enter. A broken whimper rattles from Willow. Pleasure races down my spine and sinks claws into my stomach.

"Baezal," she moans. "Please."

"So fucking tight, Willow. Tighter than before. Perfect little ass—perfect for fucking."

Her hands grip the wooden headboard as her back bows. Once I'm fully inside her, I hold still for a moment. Once her moans are more fevered, I gently pull out and thrust in firmly. She screams. My hips bounce off her ass.

Her pink hole is stretched by my gray cock. My sensitive scales skim along inside her, increasing both our pleasure. Arousal pours down her thighs and soaks the sheet below. Sweat beads along her back.

I fuck her again—in and out, over and over. Our bodies slap together in a sweet symphony. The smell of lavender over-whelmed me. She is all I feel—all I see. Her face is etched into my heart and burned into my bones. Our souls weave together, fortified by our coupling.

"Baezal," she chokes. "I'm close."

My hand sneaks over her hip, finding her greedy clit. I gently massage it as I continue to pound her.

"Come, my angel. Clench down on my cock and let me fill your ass with my seed."

I work her clit faster and faster until she erupts. I wouldn't be surprised if her screams reached shore. Pounding into her tight hole, I thrust deep and let myself follow her into pleasure. Seed rips from cock as I give her every last drop of my spend. It seeps from her little hole and flows down her legs.

Gently, I withdraw from her. Turning her trembling body on the bed, I hold her back to my chest. My wings scrape along the wooden floor of our room. I breathe in her scent and feel our hearts beating together. This is what heaven truly is. Willow in my arms with her ass filled with my come.

I couldn't think of anything much better than that.

Pressing kisses along her shoulder, Willow entwines our hands together. Silence settles in, the riotous waves lulling us to sleep. Suddenly, Willow's dark eyes open and slide towards mine.

"I thought my pussy would be your favorite," she says matter-of-factly. "Seeing as how that's the one that can get me pregnant."

My whole body tenses. The air in my lungs freezes. Willow only laughs softly before shaking her head.

"That is not some sort of declaration, my love. My womb remains empty for now." Her eyes turn wistful. "But one day, a child of our own would be perfect."

"It would be," I agree, kissing her sweaty temple. "I love you, Willow."

I was forged to protect the Sisters of the One True Faith. A servant who was cursed into stone by an evil man's dark magic. There were times throughout the century when I thought I would go mad and perish before ever being freed. I thought my soul would die encased in marble. Now, I know what it means to be alive.

Life is Willow. She is my love, my wife, and one day the mother of my children. I still do not understand how I am so fortunate as to claim her as mine. Whatever gods exist out there have blessed me beyond reason. I will strive to be worthy of such a miracle every day.

"I love you, too." A wicked gleam glistens in her brown irises. "Fuck me again so my pussy doesn't get jealous."

My bellowing laughter echoes as I do just that. The ship rocks us while I make love to her until the early hours of the morning. The true miracle will be if our simple cot survives the journey. It wouldn't be the first time I've fucked Willow on the floor.

A new town awaits us along with new adventures. My curious wife wants to see everything this world has to offer and I'm eager to oblige. While there will undoubtedly be first-time experiences, our love will always remain constant and unyielding.

More unbreakable than even the toughest stone.

A woman, offered up by her village to appease the Kraken. The merman who rescues her. A night in his palace neither one of them will ever forget. Coming March 2026!

READ ME OTHER BOOKS!

Interconnected monster romance standalone on Kindle Unlimited!

Short and spicy monster romance novellas following a different diabolical looking creature!

Holiday-themed monster romances for those who want a little extra spice on Kindle Unlimited!

ACKNOWLEDGMENTS

I want to thank all of you for picking up *A Kiss From a Gargoyle*! I hope you all enjoyed this sweet & spicy story (especially those of you whose sexual awakening was Goliath on the TV show *Gargoyles!*). Would you like to see more from Willow and Baezal? A bonus scene of them will be future in my collection book, *Kiss From a Monster Series Volume 2*, coming later this year!

I'd like to thank my beta/ARC teams, my patrons, and all of you who've shared or continue to support my work. See you in the next one!

xoxo Charlotte

ABOUT THE AUTHOR

Charlotte Swan is twenty-seven year old, living in Chicago. When she is not dreaming about being whisked away to a world filled with magic and sexy monsters, she is busy being a freelance social media marketer and full-time smut lover. To read her debut novel *Taken by the Dark Elf King*, hear about her upcoming projects, or to connect with her on social media please find her on her website or by scanning the code below.

www.authorcharlotteswan.com